DON'T
SLEEP
WITH THE
DEAD

NGHI VO

DON'T SLEEP WITH THE DEAD

TOR PUBLISHING GROUP

NEW YORK

This is a work of fiction. All of the characters, organizations, and events portrayed in this novella are either products of the author's imagination or are used fictitiously.

DON'T SLEEP WITH THE DEAD

Copyright © 2025 by Nghi Vo

A Tordotcom Book
Published by Tom Doherty Associates / Tor Publishing Group
120 Broadway
New York, NY 10271

www.torpublishinggroup.com

Tor® is a registered trademark of Macmillan Publishing Group, LLC.

The Library of Congress Cataloging-in-Publication Data is available upon request.

ISBN 978-1-250-36261-2 (hardcover)
ISBN 978-1-250-36262-9 (ebook)

Our books may be purchased in bulk for promotional, educational, or business use. Please contact your local bookseller or the Macmillan Corporate and Premium Sales Department at 1-800-221-7945, extension 5442, or by email at MacmillanSpecialMarkets@macmillan.com.

First Edition: 2025

Printed in the United States of America

0 9 8 7 6 5 4 3 2 1

for unreliable narrators
and the stories we tell

ONE

T he good thing—the only good thing—about the worst finally happening is that it has happened.

That was something the first sergeant said on the morning before the final push for Cantigny, when the sun unexpectedly rose up silver instead of gold. It was a bad omen—before the day was over, the worst came, and many men I knew did not survive it. With the situation in Europe, I found myself thinking more and more about the war, and what I came up with twenty years later and sometime after three in the morning on the edge of Prospect Park in Brooklyn, was that the first sergeant had lied.

The worst had happened, and there was nothing good about it.

The police herded us into a blind alley at the head of Tenth Street, apartments on one side and a tailor's shop on the other. It was only blank walls that faced the alley, and with the rear blocked off by a chain-link fence and the alley's mouth guarded by a pair of policemen with bristling, overeager dogs, it would be a very fine killing field indeed.

Oh come now, said a jolly voice in my head. *They certainly won't kill you. They'll take your name and your picture, and tomorrow or the next day, it'll all be out where you were and what you were doing. Perhaps they'll beat you a little, knock a club into your mouth to loosen your teeth like they did for poor old Pickett. No one's going to* kill *you, old sport, not on purpose, anyway.*

That was a voice that I had been hearing more and more as well, and it was not welcome.

There was a blizzard coming on, a few stray flakes already falling from the sky. I wrapped my wool coat more firmly around my body against the chill, but the boy next to me was shaking in a cloth jacket that was too light by far. He shrank against the brick for all that it must have been frigid, and there was a glassy look to his eyes, like a horse that had run itself wild. He was younger and poorer than usually came to Prospect Park; not unhandsome, but lost. He caught me looking at him and tried for a brave smile, but I shook my head with irritation. My teeth felt too sharp in my mouth, as if I might like to bite.

The type that usually came to Prospect Park would have taken the hint. We were mostly professionals, men with jobs that kept our hands clean. I wasn't the only columnist who took the subway across the river—I wasn't even the only one from the *Herald Tribune*. We knew how to conduct ourselves, but this boy didn't.

"Rough night," he said tentatively.

"I suppose."

"Think we can slip them some cash to look away?"

"Do you have any cash?" I asked pointedly. I didn't. I had subway fare to get back, maybe enough to pick up a sandwich on the way. Cortland from the sports desk had gotten mugged a few months ago.

He shook his head, running his bare bony hands up and down his arms.

"My ma's going to kill me," he sighed, and I looked up at the broad flat way he said *ma*, his vowels longer than anything a native New Yorker would have time for.

"St. Paul?"

"Altoona," he said, as if it should mean something to me, but it did. Altoona down by Eau Claire, just under a hundred miles from St. Paul, and I scowled reflexively.

"Are you from St. Paul?" he asked, searching my face for a sign of anything familiar. I didn't answer, instead looking up at the glass salamandrina that hung suspended from the side of the apartment building. It was about the size of a goldfish bowl, hobnailed white on the top, but clear below. They were the faddish thing when I had first come to New York in 1922, and people hung them in rows and clusters for how cheap and pretty they were. They were mostly gone now, taken down in favor of the electric lights that lined the streets with a chemical avidity. Inside the glass, the faint suggestion of a whip-tailed lizard still stirred weakly, emitting a soft mauve glow that was the next thing to invisible.

"Hey—"

"Shut up," I advised, because there was a policeman making the rounds. The alley was crowded now, at least thirty men who stood miserably alone in the mob. I recognized Perry Sloan from the attorney general's office and Henry Kent from Kent and Sons. I wondered what the Sons would make of this, reading it in the paper first thing.

Sloan had a few bills out, and the policeman was already shaking his head, insisting on the whole wallet. He would have the money in it, and Sloan's identification as well, and I idly waited to see how long it might take Sloan to figure that out. I was numb, which is different from being calm, but one was as good as the other, said the soldier bunking with the French boy and the French girl.

The war again. This was becoming unbearable, and while I do not take pride in much on the wrong side of forty, I had at least prided myself on being able to bear most things.

"Look," I said suddenly to the boy at my side. "Speak when you're spoken to. *Yes sir* and *no sir*, like you're at school. You don't know anything. You're white and young and not too much a fairy. You'll be fine."

He actually looked more alarmed at that, and I shook my head again when he started to speak.

"And for the love of Christ, don't let on that you're *with* anyone. You're alone, understand?"

He nodded, but I was already pulling away. It was only a matter of a half step to the side and a slight change of posture before it looked as if we had nothing to do with each other. God only knew there was no help in being in this together.

Sloan was looking redder by the moment, the men around him edging away. Christ, but he was going to make this worse. He never knew when to shut up, and by the looks of things, he had already had his wallet taken. As I watched, the policeman snaked his pen from his pocket as well, no doubt something terribly expensive chased with gold. Stupid as well, to have things he liked with him, and probably more out of instinct than insight, he reached to take it back.

That wasn't the way it was supposed to go, and the night tipped. What was just going to be one more dreary lot of ruined lives suddenly became something much more dangerous as the police officer drew his club and brought it down hard on Sloan's hand. Sloan's cry was shocked and sharp, and I was already drawing back from the beating I was now sure that he and whoever tried to help him were going to get.

Instead of making myself scarce against the rear of the alley, however, when I shrank farther into the shadows, the boy I had been trying to avoid speaking to earlier was there, startled at my back and tripping me up when I stumbled into him. It caused me to lurch forward straight towards the policeman's second blow, and the thought occurred, crystal-clear and tired as Armistice Day: *Well, I suppose this is what we're doing.*

I grabbed hold of Sloan's arm, dragging him back from the swinging club as it came down, and as I did so, the cry went up, police and queers all alike as we realized things weren't going the way we figured they would.

"Carraway," Sloan managed.

I let go of him, because Christ, I could never stand the man, and to hell with standing next to him any more than I had to. The police had come in force, and now they poured into the mouth of the alley while the men who had been corralled there saw a chance that they might not end the night with their lives in the trash. There were no lines, no ranks, but something broke, and suddenly the clubs were lifted and a flying rock shattered the salamandrina behind me, sending a shower of broken glass over my shoulders and plunging the alley into darkness.

Killing floor, I thought, and someone's outflung arm clipped mine, sending me backwards again. This time my heel slid on some gravel, rolling my foot neatly out from underneath me. I felt myself falling, momentarily looking up at the dimly orange sky above me, and then there was a hand clamped tight around my wrist, hauling me up to my feet again as if I had only slipped on the street.

"There, there, old sport," he said. "Just a bit of trouble, give me a moment."

Everything stopped, or everything should have stopped. The man holding my wrist let me go, but I tore after him, ignoring the shouts and the blows around me. A cry was trapped in my throat, a name. Then, next to my ear, I heard a soft laugh, and the alley went up in fire.

The flames climbed the bare brick walls, and by the sudden orange light, I saw all around me faces opened to terror. The screams started, and that reek, burned hair and burned wool, which smell just alike, filled my nose and my mouth. We stampeded towards the mouth of the alley, but we were too many, and I saw someone smashed flat against the wall, the fire catching his hair and, terribly enough, the celluloid of his glasses. They exploded off his face with a birdgun pop, and he fell under the mass of bodies trampling their way to the open air and freedom.

The fire drank the air straight out of my lungs, and for one terrible moment, I went down on one knee. I would have gone down on my face, but I threw one hand out to catch myself, and someone trod hard on my fingers, making me shout. The pain helped. It cleared away the fear in favor of something that wouldn't let me freeze. I came up, jerking my hand from under someone's boot heel, and then, almost by accident, I cleared the mouth of the alley to see men scattering in all directions as the police, some singed, tried to get them back.

The neighborhood was waking up all around us, people shouting from the windows, people screaming, and a distant clanging that would eventually summon the firemen. When I looked back, however, the fire hadn't spread, either to the apartments on one side or the tailor's shop on the other. Instead, the flames fed on nothing, collapsing in on themselves and then flaring again with magnesium white hearts. I thought I saw figures moving in the white-hot blaze, and I stared as one of the policemen snagged me by the sleeve.

That brought me back to myself, and clear on what I wanted if not clear-headed, I shoved him so he fell sprawling on the pavement, and then I ran.

The snow was falling harder now, thick wayward flakes that caught in my hair and my eyelashes without melting, but I didn't feel it. Instead something from the fire, some ember, some spark, stayed with me, burning me up from the inside, and it whispered to me, telling me that I need never be cold again, if only I would let it burn.

C H A P T E R

TWO

I don't much like to sleep, and in recent years, I had become bad at it. It was hard to fall asleep, harder to stay asleep, and hardest of all to wake up with anything like satisfaction, but after the disastrous raid on Prospect Park, I fell into my bed in my clothes. Until the sun woke me at midmorning, I dreamed badly and in fragments that made even less sense than usual. I was running. I was chasing. Someone seized the front of my shirt, dragging me forward. I was screaming, and something wanted to eat me, and then I rolled over to see the sun slipping through the blinds.

I felt strangely whole, and I stripped and showered, the hot water plentiful by this point, when my more respectable neighbors were already in church. It was Sunday, and I realized sourly that the raid had been planned that way. Saturday night raid, Sunday morning news, but when I opened my paper, there was nothing about either the raid or the fire. Across the city, there were men at their breakfast tables just as I was, swearing that they would never be so foolish or honest again, maybe looking at their wives and their children to remind themselves of what they had almost lost.

I would have lost my job, almost certainly, and it would be difficult to get another. Perhaps I would have been forced out of

New York, but that meant less to me than it might have, for all that I stayed when others left.

The Swede who cooked and cleaned for me had left a few slices of ham and a cup of mashed potatoes in the refrigerator for dinner, but I pulled them out for something to chew on as I went through the newspaper. No raid, but the paper was full of news of the war, grave accounts of alliances folding in on themselves like the wings of paper cranes, of who would come and who would not, and through it all, the tanks rolled, and the air was full of smoke and poison.

I couldn't breathe.

My hands shaking, I went to the kitchen to light the stove. It was an antique, of the type that still needed a match, and the flame leaped up as the gas took. For just a moment, my fingers lingered too close, and I pulled back hurriedly. The flames last night hadn't hurt me, I realized. These would.

Heedless of the harm, I caught the corner of the paper in the fire, and then tossed the whole smoldering mess into the sink, drawing back with a wince when it went up. The room filled with the sharp sweet smell of burning paper, and just before it was consumed by the line of orange flame, I caught the faces on the front page, delegations from a half-dozen countries come to the United States to seek aid of whatever kind might be given, and I hastily turned away.

I thought for a moment I might be sick, and then a sharp pain brought me back to myself. A spot of ash had landed on the back of my hand, and I watched in horrified fascination as it lit on my skin. There was a moment, still too long, but only a moment, where I waited to see if it would catch, if fire would prove the final lie of my existence, but instead it only stung, wasplike, before extinguishing itself. I swore absently and ran the faucet over the hurt, and the cold water hitting the burning paper sent up a billow of acrid steam.

I let the water run over the back of my hand until my fingertips were numb from the cold, and when I drew it out, the burn was only a reddened sore spot, barely even the beginning of a blister. I took a cloth from the neatly folded stack by the stove and dried my hands, and before I could quite convince myself not to, I went to my desk to flip through my address book. Some gentlemen of my acquaintance kept two, one for one life and one for another, and others left no paper trail at all. I have never had much of an imagination, and kept only one.

The operator told me she would call me back when she had my party on the line, and I busied myself at my desk as I waited for her to do so. There were the expected Christmas cards from my mother and the Minnesota cousins as well as the usual invitations to dinner or drinks. The former I put aside to deal with later because some rituals could not be forgone, not if you hailed from the better part of St. Paul, and I picked through the latter, discarding those that could be discarded and pulling out the ones that might actually be interesting. I was unpleasantly startled to see among them a letter from Ross Hennessey, who knew me from Yale, and when the phone rang, I put the missive down gratefully.

"Connecting to Paris," said the operator, and there was a hard crackle followed by a soft hiss. For a moment, I thought there had been no connection at all.

"Well, fuck you, Nicholas Carraway," said Jordan Baker.

"I see you're still angry with me." Smiling, I pulled the phone cord as far as it could go so I could sit at my desk again.

"You see correctly for once. Honestly, as if I was going to forgive you for that mess."

I imagined her as she had appeared in *Harper's* last fall, bathed in the afternoon light in her Left Bank flat, leaned so far back in her chair that it was only a miracle that kept her from tipping over entirely. When I knew her best, she'd carried herself with an athletic tension, as delicate as glass that might be shattered with one high note. On the cusp of forty, she looked stronger, her black eyes giving the camera back look for look and a sly smile on her lips. I could hear the photographer pleading with her to turn her head and gaze out the window so he could get her in dreamy profile, and I could just as easily hear her saying "Oh, I *don't* think I will" with the kind of gaiety that nevertheless meant she would do precisely what she pleased.

"I hadn't thought I did anything that needed forgiving," I said. "It's my story, isn't it?"

"It never was. Do you know that one of your friends at the *Herald Tribune* actually called me last week?"

"You know very well I don't have friends. Who was it?"

"I don't care. Someone. He pretended he forgot about the time difference to call me at three in the morning, and he wanted to know all about Daisy and Gatsby. You and Tom," she finished, "were of only secondary interest."

"And what did you tell him?"

"That I couldn't speak English," she said flatly.

I had been surprised at her English as well when I first met her at Daisy's. Tom of course hadn't prepared me for Vietnamese Jordan Baker of the Louisville Bakers, and she was so quiet at first, I thought maybe she was just a pretty ornament Daisy kept around, like the Lalique glass cat that stretched and yawned on its velvet cushion by the fire or the baby blue coupe. I hadn't said anything, talking with Tom and Daisy, who tended to command the room, and by the time I thought of Jordan again, I had made it into her good graces by saying nothing immediately idiotic. It's truly amazing sometimes, how well you can do if only you keep your idiocy to yourself.

"I'm sorry people have been bothering you," I said. "I'm still not sorry for writing the book."

"Then what is the point of calling me now?" she asked, though I could hear her making herself more comfortable.

"I missed you."

She did laugh at that, because Jordan had always liked to be missed, possibly better than she liked being liked.

"Really. Then that means you must have been doing something that you shouldn't have been. Oooh, *Nicky*, did you finally hold a boy's hand?"

I had done rather more than that last night, but I couldn't help an irritated embarrassment at her words. She wasn't twenty anymore, but she couldn't help acting like it when she was around me.

"Jordan, please."

"*Jordan, please*, what?" she asked, more sharply than she usually got with me. "After you hit the bestseller list, I should hardly think you need my permission to do anything."

I rubbed my eyes, realizing that I could crawl back into bed with very little provocation and sleep out the day.

"I saw him. I think. Last night."

There was a soft breath, followed by a flinty click. I imagined her using that heart-shaped platinum lighter she'd stolen from Daisy some twenty years ago to light her cigarettes. I hadn't smoked since that summer, for a number of reasons.

"Who?"

"Are you going to make me say it?"

"I think I had better, don't you?"

She was probably right. It was harder than I imagined it would be.

"Gatsby."

"Well. Are you all right?"

"No. Not really."

There was a tactful silence, and then she sighed.

"Well, he wouldn't be the only one. The dead are coming back over here, haven't you heard?"

"I hadn't, no."

"Read your own paper sometime. They're coming back. Old soldiers, mostly. I see them drinking at the Lièvre around the corner. They won't speak, and they reek of horseradish for some reason—"

"Not horseradish, it's mustard gas," I said automatically. "They can't speak because their throats are blistered shut."

"They're French, of course, and if it keeps up, my friends tell me we'll see the soldiers walking back from Crete and Sardinia as well. It's old magic. Gatsby's was too. You didn't mention that in your novel."

"I didn't mention a lot of things. I thought you would be grateful to me for that."

"Mm. No. I don't think I will be. But anyway, why did you call me? You can't expect me to do anything for you from all the way over here."

"I don't know. I heard him. I heard his voice or someone who sounded just like him—"

"Oh, don't do that. You know who you heard."

"I do. I heard him, and it was Gatsby dragging me up and helping me stand, getting me out of a bad kind of trouble."

"It seems there's no other kind these days," she mused. "So Gatsby's back. What are you going to do about it?"

It startled me, and I took my time answering as money burned up on the line between New York and Paris.

"I hadn't thought I was going to do anything."

"If you really think that, you wouldn't have called me. You want permission or absolution, or something like that, but I know that you aren't going to just sit there and observe, *Oh dear, I suppose Gatsby's back.* So which do you want, Nick, permission or absolution, because no one calls me to be told no."

She spoke without rancor, exhibiting that kind of patience she had only developed in recent years. It sounded good on her, or at least it was lucky for me.

"Come home," I said impulsively. "Haven't you been away from New York long enough?"

"New York's not home."

"Neither is Paris. If you stay there, you'll see more dead men, darling, and they won't be drinking at the cafes either."

I was, I knew, committing a faux pas. In conversations where the war was permitted, we spoke of almost nothing else. Jordan didn't like to have that kind of conversation, at least not with me.

"No, in New York, they spin out gossip columns for the *Herald Tribune* and write terrible books."

"I'm not dead."

"If you say so."

". . . Have a good evening, Jordan."

"Thank you, I shall."

She hung up on me with a smart click, and instead of writing my Tuesday column, I found myself looking out the window. It was snowing again or maybe it had never stopped from the night before. There had been no white Christmas this year, but perhaps we would have a white New Year's just five days from now.

I could write the column easily this evening, I told myself, standing for my coat. I could finish it and have a courier put it on Harold Greenbaum's desk before it was even late. It was Christmas with Charlie Danvers's crowd at Herons, and then the traditional midnight celebration at Marrakesh, the same crowds, the same faces, the same petty scandals. I could write it in my sleep these days, and that meant that I was free.

Free to do what? Jordan asked in my head.

Dead men weren't free, but I wasn't dead. Instead, I was made of paper, and I walked out into the winter day.

CHAPTER

THREE

The trouble, I think, began with my grandfather's brother, Leith Carraway, the patriarch of the American Carraway clan. He and my grandfather came to America almost a hundred years ago, and nearly upon arrival, he was drafted into the Civil War. Of course he would not go, not for a country where he had no roots and for slaves he might have liked to own himself, and so he found Michael Randall, a young man with a needy family living hard on the banks of the St. Croix River.

In the two-room shack with the river roaring in the spring flood, Leith Carraway used his old Sheffield razor to loosen his face from his head and traded it for another. Leith Carraway went to war for the Union and came back a hero. Randall traded my great-uncle's face back to him in return for a boat and a real house in Eau Claire, and Leith Carraway returned home to St. Paul considering it money well spent.

For many reasons, my father never liked that story, and he liked even less the story my grandmother told me on Christmas Eve when I was ten, that Leith Carraway came home from the war, and when they went to trade, something went wrong.

"It was stuck, you see. It was stuck hard and fast, and no cutting or screaming would work it loose either, and oh, Nick, my dear, they *tried*. In the end it was all blood and a dead man on the

floor with his face cut to ribbons, and your grand-uncle, why, he's
no one but Mikey Randall, trash jumped up—"

That was my grandmother's last Christmas at home before my
father sent her to live at the hospital in Grand Rapids, and I never
learned for sure which the dead man was. Whether the man who
lives in my distant memory was the well-off Englishman from
Liverpool or a fisherman's bastard from the St. Croix River, he
was Leith Carraway, and that was the end of the matter so far as
my father was concerned.

Still, I think that was where it started, the Carraway belief
that duty could be put off on someone else, and that if you only
made the right sacrifice, spilled the right blood using the right
name, that fate might be delayed or even distracted.

Two generations later, fate came calling again, and when beloved son Nicholas Carraway was called up for the first war to end
all wars, this time it was my mother's grandmother who stepped
in. I remembered her, really remembered her, her bent back, her
white hair and her old-fashioned dress. She was born in Bang-
kok, adopted or stolen by missionary parents just as Jordan had
been, and the Carraways pretended so hard and so fervently that
she was white that hardly anyone in St. Paul believed otherwise.

They summoned her from her tiny apartment in Milwaukee,
and even newly recovered from pneumonia, she came because
what other family did she have? I imagine they must have hauled
down Nick Carraway's yearbook for her, got her a map of Minnesota and pictures of the clan all together in their Sunday best.
Paper magic ran in her blood just as it does in Jordan's, and she
made me on the floor of the second-best parlor one Tuesday
morning, her shears flashing in the weak spring light as she cut
through newsprint and cardstock, snipping out hair and eyes,
hands, and muscle and bone and wit.

When she was done, I gave her a hand up, and she was so delicate, so small. They shouldn't have brought her from Milwaukee,
not as ill as she was. She was so short I had to bend to look her in

the eye, and when I did, she threw her arms around me, hugging me with a frail ferocity. She trembled, and she cried, dampening my shoulder with her tears.

"I love you," she whispered. "I love you, I love you."

Maybe she thought I would never hear it otherwise. I don't know.

They sent her back to Milwaukee. They sent their son to Canada. They sent me to muster at Fort McCoy, and against all common sense, I was the one that came back. My great-grandmother died not long after I shipped out. Nicholas Carraway was killed in a car accident two weeks after Armistice, coming back from Canada for his first Thanksgiving home.

They are gone, and I was left, and two days after Christmas, I got on the subway for the Henry Street Station. Once I arrived, I got on the train going back towards Wall Street, and then back to Henry Street Station again. I repeated the process four times, and I wondered if they had missed a payment or lost another magician. They would probably do better if they got rid of the old enchantment entirely—these days, no one cared about secrecy.

Finally, on the fourth trip, the train stopped at Columbia Street Station, which didn't rightly exist, and I stepped off to make my way to the Gates.

Back in the twenties, it had been the Lyric, and a better sort of place. Jordan had taken me there first, and I came back on my own off and on until it shut down in '34. No space goes too long empty in New York, however, and less than a year later, it opened again as the Gates. There was a pair of intricately forged iron gates mounted over the recessed door, and now it catered to a different sort of clientele. I had been a few times since the change in ownership, once with a colleague looking for information, a time or two on my own, though in the end I hadn't had the nerve for more than a few tense talks and some drinks. It was one of the last places in the city where you could get real demoniac, the demon's blood drink that had been so popular in the twenties. Demoniac puts you out of your head, lets you see ghosts and monsters, and no one could afford that kind of thing right now.

Inside the Gates was paneled with dark wood and lit with old-fashioned gas lamps. The glass shades had been removed and the gas turned up so that the flames sprouted blue and sharp, giving the whole place a lost and underwater effect. Just past noon, there were only a few patrons: a devil romancing the wife of a city alderman, another with a garishly cut throat arguing with the bartender, and two university students trying to look worldly at a table by the record player. As I had hoped, there was a jacket and hat I recognized hung off one of the far booths.

"If you're going to ask me for a favor, you should at least buy me a drink," March said, and I went to the bar. I returned with two shots of whisky, setting them down on the slick brass table before taking my seat opposite.

Agents of Hell in the United States were technically required to keep a regular face that matched their travel documents, and that face had to be human. I understood it was enforced rigorously in Washington, DC, especially when delegates came to speak before Congress, but elsewhere, the ruling was relaxed, and March looked up at me with a foxy white face, the filmy blue eyes wide and fixed, unable to focus on anything any longer. There was a smudge of dirt on his cheek, but no blood. I had shot him in the chest in 1918.

"Unkind," I said tightly.

"Really? Mostly you people love your trophies."

I was silent, and he sighed. He passed his hand over his face, drawing it forward in a sharp muzzle. When he looked up again, it was with the face of a white-tailed deer, eyes enormous in the low light and a trickle of blood dribbling from the corner of his mouth. It wasn't my memory, not quite. It was closer to something I read rather than something that happened to me. I was Nick Carraway, and Nick Carraway had killed a doe on a hunt over fall break when he was thirteen.

"Better," March judged it, and he threw back the shot because he could hardly sip it with his muzzle. "Drink. You don't come here not to drink, you know."

I did know that, and I copied his motion. For a moment, I actually wished it was demoniac. Demoniac hits me hard and dirty, though I understand it's smoother for some people. I get a rush of thick heat over my tongue, and then a feeling like falling. But demoniac reminded me that I could be anyone, and I didn't particularly want to be myself most days.

"I have questions," I said, and March set his book aside, folding his hands in front of him attentively.

"Questions this time? Not that old business again?"

I smiled at him thinly, for I did not like to be reminded of what I had asked for when I was weaker and more drunk.

"New business and old business, I think. I need to find out what happened to someone who went down."

"Go to the Society Library," March said promptly. "I'll give you that one for free, which devils never do. They have all of that information these days."

"The Society Library will tell me who went to Hell, and what year they graduated from Harvard or Yale and how long their families have been in the *Social Register*. I need to know what happened afterward."

"Whips and chains. Iron racks and molten gold poured down the throat of misers. Walking on broken legs, and walls made of screams and corridors where you walk forever with something terrible just behind you out of sight."

"I don't believe you."

"It's better if you do. You know I like you, Nick, coward that you are. You're not meant to think about that kind of thing. Your kind isn't designed for it. Think of what you could be up here instead. Rich. Powerful. Loved. Even normal."

He dangled it in front of me like a girl holding a piece of string for her kitten, and I glared at him.

"It's bad form to tell someone what they want."

There was a breath of moldering fall air clinging to his fur as he leaned in, and underneath it the acrid reek of gunpowder and woodsmoke. The doe's eyes were gelid, and I would leave a fingerprint if I touched them.

"Is that what you're doing now, beloved? Telling me what you want? That sounds like a deal."

"A small one. Nothing that would get me a place on your racks."

"Every little bit helps, said the old woman as she pissed in the sea. Ask, and we'll see how expensive I'm feeling today."

I took a deep breath. There was an unaccustomed voice in my head asking me if I really wanted to do this. I told myself I didn't, and that was a lie.

"James Gatz, better known as Jay Gatsby," I said. "I want to know what happened to him after he died and where he is now. I want to know where he's been and where he has gone."

"Oh goodness," said March, bringing his book up to cover his heart with mock scandal. "Sucking old bones, my friend?"

I realized abruptly that the book he was reading had a familiar blue cover, a pair of eyes with a runnel of green tears to the left, nude women curled tauntingly in the irises. I hissed with sudden fury, a great hand clamping around my ribs and squeezing, and I stood up from the booth, shoving the table towards him. I stepped out, but March's hand—the nails tipped black, palms utterly lineless—closed softly around my fingers.

"Sit down," he said. "Let me pull you back, and I'll spare you the embarrassment of having to find some excuse to return."

You learn, eventually, that pride and anger will not really keep you from what you truly want to do. I sat back down, but March didn't relinquish my hand, instead holding it between his and turning it over as if he wanted to read my palm. He ran his sharp fingernails along my head line and my heart line, and the doe's tongue slipped out of his mouth, red and stained with blood.

"How old are you this year?"

"Forty-seven."

"I think you are seventeen years too old to lie to yourself and pretend it's not—"

"It doesn't matter what it is," I said, and he pressed his warm hand down over mine, palm to palm and disturbingly intimate. I saw that the backs of his hands were hairless, the skin over his knuckles as smooth and unmarked as a sheet of vellum. One night, drunk, I'd met March at the Morocco and he'd put on Gatsby's face for me. I've never cared for men with Gatsby's looks. I walked away from him, and the revulsion from that little pantomime had kept me away from the Gates and from Prospect Park as well for months.

"No. I suppose not. Let me see."

His doe's eyes rolled up in an exaggerated parody of deep thought.

"What do I want from you? What do I want, what do I want."

The heat from his hand grew, going from warm to hot, and a prickle of alarm spidered up the back of my neck. There was a sting to it now, growing by the moment. I started to tug my hand away, but the doe turned her gaze to me.

"I'm thinking, Nick," he said coldly. "Let a man think."

I forced my hand to stay where it was. There were other devils, ones I knew on my own or for whom I could seek introductions, but that would take time, and none of them liked me so well as March did. He was the devil I knew, and I took a deep breath. March nodded approvingly.

"I like the book, you know. Everyone does. I think just about everyone's ready for a bit of glamour and gold after how unpleasantly gray the last few years have been."

There was no change to see. His hand didn't glow and no flames licked out from where our palms joined. Still I could see a wisp of steam drifting up, and the sting had crossed into something threatening.

"I don't think the *Times* was really fair to it. The woman came off as if she had an ax to grind. Everyone I spoke to thought it was a good read, a lovely way to pass their lunch hour."

I kept breathing through clenched teeth, every muscle in my body tensed against the impulse to jerk away. There was more steam, and I told myself I was hallucinating the smell of singeing meat. Of course I was. It wasn't that hot. It wasn't that bad. Of course it wasn't. It was fine, everything was fine.

"It was just so personal," March exclaimed. "I talked about it with your friend from the *Herald Tribune,* you know, what's his name, Greenbaum? We could hardly believe it, how personal you were."

I concentrated on breathing, air in and out. I closed my eyes, because it was better if I didn't see. I wasn't burning, I wasn't burning. I didn't have a hand. It wasn't burning. I wasn't burning. My jaw ached. I was sweating through my clothes. I wasn't burning. It wasn't real.

"Really, Nick."

March pulled his hand from mine, and my stomach lurched at the *peeling* sensation, of leaving skin behind. The pain flared up, roared, and then fell down to a fierce ache as I jerked my hand back and pulled it tight to my chest, not looking down at it. Instead I looked at March, who had taken on a human face, my face, as a matter of fact. I looked tired, dark rings under my eyes, and a drawn hardness to the set of my jaw. If someone slid their hand along the side of my face, brushed the corner of my mouth to see if I would open, I would lean into it with such relief—

He gestured to the bar, and the bartender brought me a pitcher of icy water. I scooped some ice out with my handkerchief, slopping water all over myself as I wrapped up my hand. It was stiffening already and swollen. It was the hand that had gotten stepped on the night before.

"I'd like to sneak a line into your Tuesday column," he said. "Something about Martha Ormwell at the Dagger and Garter

over Christmas. Do you think you could oblige me, if I told you
where to find out what had become of Gatsby?"

"I want you to tell me."

"I can't," he said with a shrug. "I can tell you where to find out,
though, and they will certainly answer you. You won't find them
without my direction, that's for sure."

When I hesitated, he smiled at me with my own face. It made
me look unfamiliar to myself. I had a brief moment of vanity and
a longer one of disgust.

"Come along, darling. After all, sunk cost and everything."

"All right. Tell me where to go, and I'll write up your piece."

He drew out a bone-white card, one of his own with the sigil of
a running hare printed on it in maroon, and he flipped it over to
scrawl an address on the blank side. He slid it across the table to me,
and I took it gingerly with my uninjured hand. I had seen those
cards go up in flames a time or two.

"There you are," he said. "And Nick, very good luck to you.
Looking forward to seeing what you write next."

He opened my book again, still wearing my face, and I thought
of my great-uncle Leith's Sheffield razor, sliding along the point
of March's jaw, peeling back the skin and shearing it from the
bone. After all, I thought, it was *my* face.

Instead I turned and walked away, still clutching my burned
hand to my chest. The two university students stared at me, a little green around the gills, and I pushed past them and the throat-
cut devil, who moved to accost me, a hyena after wounded prey.

"I'm *done*," I said hoarsely, shouldering by him, but even as I
made it past the iron gates, I very much doubted it.

The snow had stopped, and it was that crystalline hour that
winter days got, when everything is so clear it aches. I took several deep breaths and peeled the wet handkerchief back from my
hand. The skin of my palm was swollen and painfully red, some
spots darker than others, speckled a deep crimson. There was one
spot, the worst, on the fleshy pad below the thumb, that had split,

and from that spot drifted the smell of singeing paper as well as burned meat. The white skin peeled back, fluttering a little in the sudden gust of wind, and in the split I saw words, neat lines of black print on white, before I closed the handkerchief over it too hard, my stomach rebelling entirely as I threw up on the sidewalk.

C H A P T E R

FOUR

I returned home on foot, the shadows crowding at my heels and the sounds of the city after Christmas oddly muted. There was something subdued about Manhattan in the week between Christmas and New Year's, I thought, not for the first time. It wasn't real, or perhaps it was dead. Nothing we did mattered.

My flat felt as cold inside as it was out, and I kept my coat on as I got the radiator turned up and went to the bathroom to tend to my hand. I ran cold water over it, as icy as I could get, and then I could stand to look at it more closely, using a pair of sharp scissors to snip away the loose skin and bare the wound for better healing. It struck me as I looked over the injury, the print at the deepest part turned blurry and smudged with fluid, that it was a hopeful thing, tending to your wounds, assuming you would be around to enjoy a time after they healed.

I threw away the fouled handkerchief and applied a layer of Dakin's solution to my hand, sealing it with petroleum jelly before applying a gauze bandage. It would hold, and reluctantly, I went to sit down at my typewriter. The fingers of my left hand could bend somewhat, but too much movement sent a nasty shudder of pain through my arm up to my elbow. Finally, I simply pecked slowly at the keys with my right hand alone, cursing quietly and crossing out nearly as many words as I kept. Herons,

Marrakesh, and now the Dagger and Garter as well, with Martha Ormwell in attendance. Given that I had been drinking too much just like everyone else, even the parties I was there for had to be half made up: who was there, who conspicuously wasn't, and what was done and to whom. There was a desperation to the whole scene, as if we could feel the world tipping out from underneath us again, and if we only laughed loudly enough, danced long enough, and kept our eyes shut, it would stay as it was. So there, Martha Ormwell was at the Dagger and Garter, along with a half dozen other names that I guessed at, and I pulled the page from the roller with an angry snap.

By then, it was almost full dark outside, and the single lamp lit on my desk formed a feeble barricade of light. The pages felt oddly heavy in my hand. As I jammed them clumsily into an envelope, I thought that this would be the last time I wrote for the *Herald Tribune*, that one way or another, it was over.

Then I shook my head, because I had had feelings like that before, many times, and most often, almost always, they meant nothing at all.

I called for the courier service, and then I took March's card out of my wallet where it waited like a particularly discreet bit of poison. It was malice, and of course it was self-destruction. Devils in New York didn't trade in anything else, and they don't do anything for free. Still there are some poisons that you can only drink from your own hand. Pain endured did not justify pain to come, and already I had the idea that no matter what I found at that address, what infernal machinery, what slaughterhouse, it would be painful. It would hurt, and as March knew, I was a coward. I could not stand to be hurt.

The buzzer, brassy with an insectile accent to the ring, made me jump, and I slid the card under the foot of my typewriter, going down to hand over my article.

That night, I dreamed again of a place of mist, and though I could not see, I knew that the ground could at any moment open up under my feet, and I would fall. When I awoke, March's card was crumpled in my burned hand.

When I was younger, I preferred to walk when I was in the city, covering long distances simply because I had the time and the inclination. These gray days, the sidewalks were more crowded, and there were more men without a place to go. I liked it less now, and after I was dressed and had bought a cup of coffee from the place around the corner, I ended up hailing a cab.

The cabbie didn't blink at the address, but New York cabbies didn't flinch from anything, and I had no idea where we were going until we pulled up outside the Queens General Hospital in Hillcrest. The campus had only been dedicated four years ago, and even under the flurry of snow and the darkening sky, it bustled with people going about the business of life and pre-serving it.

"Is this right?" I asked, and the cabby gave me a dire look without responding. Of course it was, and I paid him, getting out into the cold midmorning.

I lurked around the entrance, wondering how credible it would be to simply go in and ask for the resident devils, and I could hear March laughing in my head. I lingered long enough that one of the security guards started to approach, but then a large family, easily a dozen adults with children in tow came in, all crying out and shouting for some unfortunate relative, and I attached myself to them, getting past the lobby of the main building and into the heart of the place.

Queens General was a painfully modern institution, a public hospital with the starched uniforms and harsh light that were rolled out every time someone wanted to know what the city had done for the indigent poor. Nothing like salamandrinas here; it was all electricity, grounded and run off generators and backup generators that could keep the place going for years.

It was still a hospital, however, and there was a vaguely haunted air to the halls, especially when I got away from the public areas and into the administrative portions, mostly underground. They'd kept the old foundations of the original buildings, the same warren of tunnels, and here, against all sense, it was still run on gas. While the floors above were practical linoleum, down here they were tiled, an extravagant pattern of green ferns bordered in a Greek key design. It was the kind of thing everyone but the rich had stopped doing once the Depression hit, and it was funny to find it in the dark, between the old hospital records and the supply rooms.

Once or twice, some orderly or clerk gave me a fleeting frown, but if you are a white man of indifferent looks, you can walk for a long time without being stopped, if you only do so quickly.

Still I was walking quickly without purpose before I looked down and saw that the tiles underneath my feet had changed. The green fern pattern had shifted, and at first you might be excused for thinking it simply the effect of a misplaced row of tiles or a trick of the light. The farther I walked, though, the more pronounced the deformation became. The fern fronds grew longer and more sinuous, their curves taking on a menacing, grasping aspect. They overwhelmed the Greek key design that was keeping them in, and they swarmed first to the sides of the corridor and then to the walls, and then up them.

The gaslights flickered unreliably, and it came to me that I had been walking too long. I would probably be under the Jamaica Train Yard by now if this were some normal place, but of course it wasn't. Among the twisting ferns, I caught shapes like eyes, watching me, and when I paused to look at them, they closed just a half second too slow for me to think they were imaginary.

"I could always leave," I said out loud, touching the tile where a pair of eyes had been. It was slightly clammy under my fingertips, sweating out the chill.

Of course you could, old sport, but then you would never find out, would you? What a bore.

"You can't goad me into doing what you want. That kind of bait doesn't work on me anymore."

Whatever you like. But I will tell you that we've never done anything together that you didn't want to do. Not really my style, even if I suspect it might be yours.

I started to walk again, imagining his smile just behind my shoulder. If I turned back, I would see it disappearing into the ferns.

"Tell me. Are you speaking to me, or is this only my imagination? If I summoned you up from the dead to speak, this isn't what I want you to say."

Oh? What do you want me to say, then?

I had written a good half dozen novels over the years, along with the column and the most recent book that had Jordan so cross with me. I wasn't bad—I made enough money that in addition to my inheritance I could keep myself fairly well even after '29. The problem of course was that anyone who tells other people stories first must tell themselves stories. I had been telling myself stories for a long while about Gatsby, and now I no longer trusted them, either his voice in my head or who I knew him to be.

The ferns curled up towards the ceiling, and I became aware of the churn and thud of heavy machinery. At Queens General, it would be the turning of the generators, but of course, it wasn't anything like that here. Instead, it was some kind of distant mechanism of unknown purpose, and it came to me as I walked that it would hide other noises, like shouting or screaming, like footsteps. I walked faster.

The rise and fall of the engine was irregular, no beat exactly as long or as short as any other. I would walk in time with it without thinking for a few moments, and then abruptly miss a step. I was off stride, and every time I caught myself up, it seemed as if the engine's pulse beat just a little louder. I was getting closer, and a sick dread filled my belly.

"I can turn around any time I want to," I said out loud. "I could leave you wherever you are now. You would never have come looking for me."

This time, Gatsby or the imagined Gatsby who spent so much time in my head, didn't reply, and instead of turning around, I kept walking. It occurred to me that I had no idea if turning around would take me back the way I had come. There were places in the world where it wouldn't, and Queens General Hospital, or the place that you could get to from there, might have been one of them.

The engine acquired a terrible buzzing sound, as if a belt had slipped, and that noise filled my ears. There was a whine to it, something that planted itself at the back of my neck and rose up towards my temples, and it made me think of things I couldn't escape, the smell of blood and mud and cordite.

The fern fronds had taken over the corridor now, and between the thin curling leaves, there were shapes moving, separated from me by less than a whisper of green. The corridor grew darker, grew closer, and at last I broke into a run, because when something is behind you and you cannot face it, you can run or you can fight, and I knew where fighting got you, had known for a generation or more.

I ran with the shadows of claws reaching out beyond the ferns to pluck at my hair and my clothes, ran until my breath burned in my lungs and my legs ached, ran until I hit a damp patch on the tiled floor—and then with a startled cry, I slipped and fell towards the tile with dangerous speed. I threw my hand out to catch myself, the bad one, and the pain shooting up from my burned palm was hot enough to clear my mind of everything but a blank white agony. All I could do was roll on my back, groaning and with my hand curled to my belly. Almost as if they had never been, the claws retreated and the eyes that had been watching my panic with avid interest closed.

After a moment I registered that I was stretched in front of a plain wooden door, unmarked and unremarkable. I looked up and down the hallway, which was, now I could see, just another hallway. I thought that perhaps I could even hear the administrative clatter of the hospital somewhere. It occurred to me that it was a little like the Gates. The way to the Gates and to this particular door wasn't distance but a price. The Gates were paid with a waste of your time, and here, it was paid with fear. I got to my feet and listened at the door, hearing nothing beyond but two voices conversing quietly.

I knocked, and when several long moments went by without an answer, I knocked again, more loudly.

"Come in," came an irritated woman's voice, and I opened the door.

It was any dreary lawyer's office with its glass case of self-important books and a row of filing cabinets along the side. There were a pair of windows as well, the blinds pulled down, and behind the desk, a single white woman seated with a thick spread of papers arrayed in front of her. She was stout and dressed in a fantastically tailored gray checked dress. When I stepped closer, I saw that except for her dress, she was all the same substance, her hair, her skin, her eyes and her lips.

"It's wax," she said abruptly.

"I beg your pardon—"

"I'm wax. I was an anatomical beauty in Genoa, originally."

She must have taken my confusion for interest, because she winked slyly and undid the bow at her collar, pulling it down to show me that below her collarbones, she had no skin. It was only a blandly red expanse, muscle that had been carved with hairline striations to indicate how they would stretch and flex. I was lightheaded, as if I had been suddenly thrown up into the air and forgotten which way was down, my mouth sticky and dry.

"Do you like it?" she asked confidentially, loosing another button. "I would let you touch."

"No. No."

I shook my head numbly, and with a shrug, she did up her dress again, tying her bow with a neat flourish and taking up her cigarette from the tray by her side. The ember at the end of her cigarette glowed an unhealthy red, mimicking, I realized, the impossible light that leaked in through the blinds. We were deep underground, and suddenly I was very grateful that the blinds were down.

"What a pity. I thought as you are—well. No matter. What do you want?"

I stared at her eyebrows because then I wouldn't have to look into her eyes, which were fixed and unmoving.

"I need to know what happened to Jay Gatsby. He died in 1922. He made deals with Hell, and I want to know what happened to him afterward and where he is now."

She made no move, not towards the papers in front of her or the filing cabinets behind her. She took another puff from her cigarette and looked at me without curiosity.

"You must know devils don't do anything for free."

"What do you want?"

"Stay here with me. I'd love to pin you to my wall."

"No. He's not worth that."

I mostly believed it.

She made a moue. She didn't really think I would go for that, but I could see that like any saleswoman on commission, she had to try.

"Well, how about since I showed you mine, you show me yours?"

I stared blankly at her. The first thing I thought was that she was attractive, the second thing was a slight shock at how long it had been since I was naked in front of anyone.

"You just want me to take my clothes off? And you'll tell me what I want to know?"

"Oh, I just think your shirt will do. But, yes. I'll tell you what you need to know."

She gestured for me to lean back against her desk as I shed my coat and my jacket before unbuttoning my shirt and vest, and she winked at me as she came around. When she moved, it was more clear than ever that she was made of wax, wax that lived, wax that could bend, but wax nonetheless. She smelled like beeswax dripped for generations on a stone floor. Her cheek had the translucence of a burning votive, and she held a pair of crooked surgical shears in her hand.

"You probably shouldn't look," she said, and dutifully, I turned my eyes up to the ceiling, flinching when I saw a woman half-grown into the tiles up there. Her head, shoulders, and one arm were free, and her long dark hair hung down towards me. I had no idea how I had missed her before, when the ends of her hair were barely a foot above my own head. She blinked slowly at me, one eye faster than the other, and the former anatomical beauty snipped at my undershirt, baring my skin to the chill of the air.

Above me, the woman in the ceiling moved her lips, her mouth opening and shutting with a viscid slowness. I had heard her talking as I came in, so she obviously could. This felt like something else.

Something sharp slid along my sternum, from my throat to my navel and then back again, and I hissed as she pressed deeper. It was a dull kind of pain, the insertion of a needle after the dentist had numbed your gums. It hurt, and it was made worse by knowing that it should have hurt much worse. I stared up at the woman in the ceiling, taking in the oval of her face, the hard cuts of her cheekbones. The anatomical beauty put her shears down, picked up her cigarette again. The tip was too close to me, and I held my breath against the fear of pain and incineration.

There was a brief whirring sound, something so familiar that my brain tried to tell me that of course it wasn't what I thought it was, not in this strange place. The woman in the ceiling tilted her head back and forth, her mouth opening and shutting. I wondered who she had been before, and it came to me that that sound was the buzz of pages being bent back and then loosed in a fan, the paper shuffling out from under your thumb. I stared harder at the ceiling as the anatomical beauty laughed softly.

"How honest," she said, almost to herself. "At least, you like to think you are."

Not anymore, I might have protested, but the whirring continued, with pauses that felt like a yawning void opening up under my breast bone. Her hands were busy, and I was afraid that if I looked down, I would see them at some kind of surgery that I would never be able to forget.

The woman in the ceiling stared down at me, and I tried to imagine sympathy in her face, or perhaps hatred or fury, anything but the blistering indifference I suspected. Her eyes were large and liquid, calm as a saint's before immolation.

The anatomical beauty's breath grew high and soft. She giggled, a sound like a handful of steel tacks dropped on the floor, and then she stepped away from me, stubbing her cigarette in the tray and taking out a handkerchief to daintily wipe her fingers.

"You can get dressed now," she said, returning behind her desk, and gratefully, I looked away from the woman in the ceiling. When I didn't look at her, it was astonishingly easy to forget she was there, and I did up my buttons over the ruined undershirt. I had my coat back on by the time the anatomical beauty came up with a file from her drawer. It was thin, and when she opened it, I saw that there was only a single sheet of carbon paper inside.

"Eaten," she said at once, and when my stare grew louder, she glanced up at me with a touch of impatience.

"Eaten," she repeated. "It doesn't get more clear than that, does it?"

There was a wind howling through my head, midnight on the field and moonlight setting a sniper's paradise.

"That's not enough. There must be more. When? How?"

"Do you mark down every sandwich you eat?" she asked.

"When, some eight years ago. How, someone opened his mouth and bit, and that is that, my dear."

Her enjoyment was made all the worse by the look of false pity she wore, her smile solicitous, her wax teeth flashing in the low light.

"I saw him," I said hollowly. "Two nights ago, by Prospect Park. It was him."

"It is very easy to think so," she said with understanding. "What we consume becomes ours, doesn't it? Someone took his face and his manner, probably his memories as well. I'm sure they were very good. Someone ate his life, Mr. Carraway, and I am afraid there is no resurrection from the upper intestine."

The reality of it hit me somewhere low in my body. I had managed to eat some toast and ham that morning. Now I wished I hadn't because I could feel its weight inside me, and it was like there was a rope between my temples, pulling ever tighter until my skull should crack.

"Are you going to be sick?" she asked curiously. "Is your heart breaking?"

Not in front of you, I thought.

"Miss, you are enjoying yourself too much," I managed, and I stepped out of her office. As I turned, I caught out of the corner of my eye the reaching hand of the woman in the ceiling, and there was a plasticity to her limbs or they were longer than they had looked at first glance. She managed to graze my shoulder with a fingertip, trying to catch me, trying to comfort me, I never knew which.

I slammed the door behind me, and I started to walk. The tile was an exuberant pattern of ferns and nothing more, and soon enough, I returned to the Queens General Hospital, because surely that was not where I had been.

"Sir," said a nurse with some alarm, "sir, sit down, you're not well."

I shook my head, pulling away from the gravity of her care. It was snowing outside, and this time there was a violence to it, the white and the wind. I started walking. I wasn't sure when I was going to stop.

CHAPTER

FIVE

didn't sleep at all that night. I paced my apartment because leaving it felt dangerous. The whole world felt dangerous, less stable than a film of oil over water. I realized that I was staying away from my windows sometime around two, and impatient with myself, I went to throw open the blinds in defiance of what my old fears insisted.

The snow was piling up to blizzard proportions, and the lights outside, electric, yellow and lifeless, gave the street a dull sodium cast. This was the world, and I was offended I was living in it. Even beyond the confines of my apartment it was too small, too cramped. Everything was after Gatsby, and quieter as well, less vivid, less bright.

I must have fallen asleep at some point, because I woke up to a call from one of my many aunts. Before I was awake enough to deny her, I found myself agreeing to meet up with someone from St. Paul fresh to New York for the new year. It was easier than saying no, though I hardly felt that way after another hour of fitful sleep.

I shaved with care, but I still cut myself rather badly in doing so. Out of a morbid curiosity, I arched my neck, angling towards the mirror. I spread the sides of the wound open, creating a yawning stinging sensation that sickened me. Still I didn't let go, examining the split skin even as blood welled up and streaked down my neck. Just red, just flesh, no words, but what words would I expect to see there anyway?

Before I could think about what I expected to see beneath my skin, I cleaned the wound, and then cleaned and rebandaged my burned hand as well. I was racking up quite a number of injuries before the end of 1939, I mused, and for some reason, I thought I wasn't done yet.

Eventually, I pulled my mind back to its track, and I dressed and was halfway to the automat on Seventh Avenue when I realized who I was meeting.

The name Ross Hennessey meant a few things to me. It meant Ross Hennessey of the St. Paul Hennesseys, who had been in the region two or three generations longer than the Carraways. Carraways and Hennesseys went to the same church, they ate together, they raised their children together, they made the same decisions about who was clever and who was an upstart. Nick Carraway grew up with Ross Hennessey, but of course I hadn't.

Ross Hennessey also meant Yale, memories that weren't mine of a boisterous campus and young men doing what young men liked away from the eyes of their families. Ross Hennessey meant studying at the library, beer in town, and other things that were less than nothing to me.

The distaste I felt for Hennessey was somewhat akin to finding a shirt left unwashed under the bed, something discarded, and even if it had been missed once, that had passed once you observed how filthy it was and unpleasant.

And still, despite that, I went anyway, because right now, I could not stand to be alone—eaten, he was eaten, and how would that have felt? I didn't want to imagine it, and at the same time, I couldn't stop myself from trying—and every person in New York was like any other. It might as well be Hennessey as anyone else.

The automat on Seventh, as I understood it, had been around

since the pandemic. Some man from Belgium remembered the idea from home and quickly made a fortune off the people in the apartments that didn't have their own cook stoves. It never regained the wild fortune of a time when between two hundred and four hundred people were dropping dead in New York every day, but it did a brisk business until the crash, when the owner shot himself in the alley behind the kitchen. It could have become a proper restaurant or a gallery or a hardware store, but instead it stayed just as it was, eking out a thin existence serving up lukewarm food and other things to the exhausted, the insomniac, and, of course, the tourists.

On a weekday after the lunch hour, it was mostly empty. Somewhere behind the wall of shoebox-sized compartments, there was presumably a staff that put out fresh food and hopefully removed the stale, but besides them, there were just a handful of lingerers, and, peering into one small window after another, a tall man with his coat over his arm. I recognized him, after a fashion. It came up for me coldly, the words *That is Ross Hennessey. We were friends in St. Paul* scrolling across my mind like a movie marquee.

I shook it off and put on a practiced, pleasant smile. I could put up with forty minutes of pleasantries with a friend from home. I thought I could put up with forty minutes of anything.

"Hello, Hennessey—"

I made a strangled sound as he cried my name like a stuck pig, coming over to pound me on the back in eager goodwill. The other patrons of the automat gave us suspicious looks, and I noticed in an absent kind of way that the woman in the hairy tweed coat had hair that was made of very fine feathers, a buttery gold color that looked painfully artificial in the winter light. It had been in vogue years ago, and the pinfeathers got everywhere, clinging to your clothes as you went about your day.

Up close, Hennessey was attractive in a debauched kind of way. He had been a fantastically handsome man at Yale, and now he could coast on its remnants. It allowed him to look louche rather than ruined, and he had enough natural charm to keep it going.

"It's splendid to see you, Carraway! My God, what's it been, twenty years?"

"At least that long," I said with a reluctant smile. "Hard to imagine."

"Here, let me get you some lunch, since you were so kind as to come—"

I remembered that Middle Western dance at least, and after some shuffling, I won the dubious honor of paying for the privilege of feeding us both. Obscurely proud of myself for getting it right, I fed a few coins into the slot, pulling out a warm chicken plate for me and a somewhat monstrous pasta dish for him. As I removed the plates, I saw a glimpse of movement through the smoked glass that led to the rear of the automat, someone moving beyond. It was an oddly comforting thing, that there was still someone there.

I settled us at a table by the door, and I listened as Hennessey chattered between bites of food, about people we had known and things that I was fairly certain we had actually done. I picked at my food to keep from finishing too much before he did, and it came to me as he spoke that there was something frenetic about him, and something afraid. He smelled acrid, and the collar of his shirt was yellowed with sweat. I am a good listener, famous for it by now, but he couldn't seem to get the reaction he wanted from me, no matter what angle he tried.

Finally he rocked back in his chair, giving me a puzzled and exasperated look. We were now alone in the automat, and he didn't bother to keep his voice down.

"So what is it about you?"

I gave him a placid look, because I was reaching the point when I could politely leave. He had actually served his purpose rather admirably—I now wanted to be alone more than almost anything.

"What is it about me?" I echoed.

"You wrote this book. More than just writing it, you sold it. You put it on the street, and anyone who wants to can read it."

"I hope they do. My rent rather depends on it."

He laughed harder at that joke than it deserved, the sound bouncing off the automat's tiled walls like an animal trying to get out.

"My God, the rent in this city! You know, I thought of moving out here before the crash? It would have been, oh, what, '25, '26? You weren't here then, were you? I heard that you were back out West for a while."

"Yes, I was trying out Los Angeles. There was a woman out there," I said vaguely. "I moved back here just before the crash."

"Rotten luck," he said with a bad attempt at sympathy. "I saw the rents at that point, and I never realized it could be so expensive just to live and to eat, and to do both so poorly. Like this place. I thought, I don't know. It might be magic, or something similar to it."

It probably would have been two decades ago, the ability to pull nearly anything out of the drawers that you could imagine or that you might deserve. During the twenties, New York was a place where you could pull out all kinds of wonder just by dropping a quarter in the slot. I smiled pleasantly.

"It's a kind of magic to get what it is you want, isn't it?" I asked, nodding at our food, and he must have thought I was offended because he went into an earnest tirade about what he meant, and how much he liked the city, both now and when he was younger, no matter how expensive it was. By then, I was starting to see the shape of things, so that when he leaned back from his empty plate, tapping two fingers with an unlit cigarette between them on the table, I was unsurprised.

"Look," he said. "I don't know what you know about how I've been doing back home."

"Nothing at all," I promised him, and he smiled as if I had done him a special favor rather than steadfastly dropping my aunts' letters into the trash.

"But anyway, things haven't been so very easy. My father retired last year, and now it's just me and old Pelham in the office, mostly handling piddling things. You know, small claims, nothing worth anything."

I started to say that it was a shame, that things had been difficult for a long time, but he reached across the table to pluck at my sleeve. The gesture, oddly childlike, made me pause, and he offered a smile that I understood he had used on the girls at Yale all the time, half-shy, half-winsome, devastating to a certain kind of young woman who wanted to be understanding, and just a little nauseating to me now.

"What I'm saying, Nick, is that I could use a little help getting by. Your book came out, the local paper ran a feature on it—"

"No one in town was putting a pig in a dress that week?" I inquired, and then I made a face because that was needlessly cruel. "I'm sorry, but—"

"Not much," he said, coaxing. "Just five hundred. I just need five hundred to crawl out of this hole."

I couldn't stop myself from laughing incredulously, rising from the table.

"That's more than it costs me to live in a year. It was good to see you. Give my regards to your family, of course, but, no."

I turned to go, but he stood and came after me. If I had thought that good manners would protect me from any of this, I was wrong, and the problem, one peculiar to the Midwest, I have observed, is that once we have worn through our manners, what is left is something much rawer and more ugly.

"Not even five hundred," he persisted. "Four hundred. It won't fix anything, but my God, Nick, it would mean so much. I'm a married man now, and I know you don't know what that's like, but let me tell you."

"Thank you, no," I said sharply, stepping out of the door into a gust of wind. It was already getting dark, and the snow, piled up on the hoods of the parked cars and the lampposts, distorted the light in strange ways.

"You know I wouldn't ask if I didn't need it."

"Why would you even ask, then? Hennessey. I am telling you no, not now, and not in the future. I am sorry. You should go home. As you said, New York is so very expensive, isn't it?"

He drew up short at my savagery, as I hoped he would, and I walked away from him down the street. New York, I supposed, had been good for me in that respect—if I were in Chicago or St. Paul, that would easily have taken twice as long.

Instead of letting me go, however, Hennessey lunged forward, a moving blur out of the corner of my eye. I half turned in alarm, but instead of striking me in the face or the back of the head as I guessed he very much wanted to do, he grabbed me by the back of my coat like a recalcitrant hound, hauling me into the alley behind the automat. We were concealed from the alley's mouth by a dumpster, and the alley ended nearly flush to another building. *A man killed himself here,* my brain offered, as if trying to entertain me in this moment.

I tried to shake Hennessey off, but my feet slid in the slush as he slammed me with bone-jarring force against the brick wall.

"Nick," he said, half-pleading. "My life is over if I can't get out of this. Do you understand? My life is *over.* I might as well put a bullet in my head if I can't get out of this."

I was faintly shocked by the fact that I didn't much mind the sound of that, even when the raw brick was biting into my shoulders.

"Surely it's not as bad as all that. You could—"

"You think I haven't?" He laughed, an ugly sound that made me realize, more than anything else had, that he was serious.

There is a golden sheen that sits over my memories of St. Paul, for all that they are not really mine. It insists that the Midwest is more genteel, more innocent, but of course that is a lie. You could destroy yourself anywhere. You could kill yourself anywhere.

"I've made the rounds in St. Paul," he said, almost normally, almost as if he wasn't holding me to a brick wall behind a dumpster. "And after that, I went down to Chicago, and to my wife's family in Cincinnati. Do you fucking know what a thing it is, to go begging favors from your wife's father? Of course you don't. But I went, and I begged—"

"And I don't care," I said, trying to shove him back, but he leaned his weight in, slamming me against the wall hard enough that I struck the back of my head on the brick. I bit back a cry, hanging on to his wrists. If only I could get my feet underneath me, but the slush prevented it, kept me half-hanging on to him for support.

"No, you don't, do you?" Hennessey asked, as disgusted as if he weren't begging me for a favor. "But you will care if anyone finds out what you did that summer."

I was only listening with half an ear. If I could get my feet underneath me, to hell with fighting fair, but now something in his voice made me pause, glaring at him through the swirl of snow.

"That got your attention," he murmured, his tone growing quiet. "You haven't forgotten, have you? That I was there?"

"What the hell are you talking about?"

He got a jagged smile on his face, like someone had slid a knife into the side of his mouth and pulled violently.

"Anders's father got us all out of it, and Anders and Gunderson will keep mum, but I don't have to, do I? It was me there with you."

There was something stirring inside my head, a sensation like the scrape of a very narrow thin knife over paper. A bookseller I'd met years ago had told me about it, how you might apply tiny patches of paper over mistyped or miswritten text with a pinhead's worth of glue. The fix might be so invisible that only the most delicate scraping would reveal the error underneath, and too frantic a search would destroy it altogether.

"It was me," Hennessey insisted as if I had tried to deny him, and an animal fear woke up in me. Whatever he was going to tell me, I could tell I didn't want it, didn't want to be threatened with it, but more didn't want to know it.

I swore, pushing away from the brick wall. It was enough to throw him off balance, almost enough to get me away, but he grabbed me around the chest from behind and heaved me back. Then we were both slipping, and he twisted so that we landed in the plowed-up snow, already up past our shoes and so cold it burned against my skin. I flailed to gain my feet, and this time if I had, I would've given him a hard kick to keep him down if I thought it might win me free, but Hennessey, damn him, was faster.

One hand against my throat thrust me back against the ground, and then he heaved his weight on top of me, coming to throw one leg over my chest and settle his weight over me. It forced the breath out of me, and he leaned down. In the fading light, I could see the whites of his eyes, like a dog about to bite. He smelled like sweat, and now that I was so close, of alcohol as well, something that came through his skin as well as his breath.

"You remember her, don't you? How she wouldn't stop crying? She wouldn't stop crying with her nose all bloody, and that was you, and you *laughed*."

I shook my head wildly, because I didn't remember, and neither did the man for whom I was sent to war. I would have known such a thing, I would never forget such a thing, it would mark me for my entire life, shame and self-disgust and guilt and horror, but of course *he* forgot, so I had.

That patch was peeling up now, scraped up, gouged up, and

I could see a name, Daphne Blackwood, and a boathouse half-hidden by a stand of cottonwoods.

Hennessey's hands knotted in my shirt, something ripping as they tightened and shook me.

"We walked away, we all did, and we'd all go down now if I told, but do you think it matters to me anymore? It doesn't, and if my life is over, then, well, so's yours, you son of a bitch. They fished her out of the river with a baby inside her, and no one forgets that kind of thing, and maybe they'll remember me, poor failure, but they'll remember you for sure, big author, fucking—"

I could barely feel him on top of me now because under the dry scrape of a thin-bladed knife, I could see another winter, home from school. An unlucky girl and four men, *Jesus,* who thought themselves very lucky indeed. It was me, and it wasn't, and if I could have shed my skin to be rid of that kind of dirt, I would have gone after it with a Sheffield razor.

Hennessey was still speaking, still spitting his words into my face, but what was worse was that boathouse on the water, and what I had done because I didn't see a way for Daphne Blackwood to stop me. There's no such thing as forgetting, not really, and Nick Carraway never had. Instead he had done the next best thing for a man like him, which was pretend to forget, until eventually he could forget to pretend, and he became a man who had never raped a sixteen-year-old girl on the banks of the Rum River.

My hands fell off of Hennessey's wrists, and a crushing weight came down over my chest. My vision narrowed until all I saw was his contorted face over mine, and briefly and clearly it came to me, *This must be what Hell is, this knowing, and this lack of breath and this man on my chest choking the life out of me.*

Suddenly the pressure decreased, granting me one swift breath of freezing cold air, and then it dropped on me again harder than before, hard enough that my sternum creaked and with it came a thick brilliantly red rain that hit my face and my hair with a flat, final splatter.

I turned my head away instinctively but not before it stung my eyes and a few stray drops ended up on my lips. I gagged, but Hennessey was lifted off of me, and a pair of hands took me firmly by the elbows, hauling me up with such strength that I had no option but to stand.

"There. That could be worse, couldn't it?"

It was no voice that I recognized, flat as the knock of a fist on a pineboard coffin.

I did recognize the face, that of the demon with the cut throat from the Gates. Up close, he was nearly exactly my height, but heavier in build, wider through the shoulders and all of it carried with the kind of tension that kept dancers on bleeding pointe.

I froze. His eyes were the only living thing in his face, yet I didn't need to see them to know him. My body somehow knew him before I did, but that was wrong. I had always known.

I gagged again at the slick taste of rancid copper, jerking my head back. He turned from me and advanced on Hennessey, who was, against all belief, still alive, thrashing in the stained snow. The only sound he could make was a distant mountain whistling—his windpipe was severed.

I started forward, not sure what I was going to do, but it was the devil who looked over his shoulder at me, nothing human, never human, and my nerve broke into a thousand pieces.

I ran out from the alley into the snow. Every moment, I expected a policeman's whistle, a sensation of burning, the eyes in the shadows to open, but there was nothing, and I only ran.

C H A P T E R

SIX

There was a bloody streak on the side of my face, marking his touch. Even in the darkness no one could mistake it for anything but what it was, not as thick as it dripped, and then I had to get it off my skin, at once. Of the man who had put it there, I could not think at all, and instead I concentrated on the blood, because after all, there was so much of it.

That's evidence, I thought in the shower, long after the last of the red had swirled down the drain. I stepped out of the tub, drying myself like it was any other night, and I concentrated on how real everything was and how familiar, because if I didn't, I would see the devil again, and I would start to shake.

Hennessey was no devil, however, and when I thought of him, I found myself curiously indifferent. I tried to find some hint of terror or pity for him, but there was none. It might come later, I thought, or like so many things, it might not come at all. Kindness was never promised, and neither was sympathy.

When I thought about Daphne Blackwood, however, the horror came, as well as the panic and the sorrow and the guilt. It struck like a storm, in waves, and all I could do was think that if I had his money and his face and his family, then I must have this too, the memory of her face under my knuckles, and what came afterward and the after that must have kept on coming for her, even when Nick Carraway was safely back at school and living a life that had no part of this.

I realized sometime after midnight that I could do what he had done. I could plaster it over and put it away as well, and it would never trouble me any more than it had troubled him. I wouldn't know, and the people who did, they could never hurt me. For me, it might be nothing more than a story written on cheap paper and left in the rain to wilt and dissolve.

It made me think, suddenly and with the power of a camera lens snapping into focus, of the devil who had saved me, or rather, who had murdered Hennessey. There was no telling how long he had been standing there in the alley with us, watching us, listening to Hennessey speak.

Around dawn, I called my mother. When the sleepy maid summoned her to the phone, she said my name cautiously, like a question. She knew very well who I wasn't, but she still answered.

"Is there. That is. Is there a Blackwood family? That we know?"

"No, not at all," she said, and then almost immediately, "Wait, I believe there was, wasn't there? Something up north, Mary Beth, do you remember?"

I listened to her confer with the maid for a short while, and when she came back, she was more sure.

"There's a Blackwood who became a teacher at the high school here, just a few years behind you. Is that who you are thinking of?"

"Maybe. Tell me, please, was there a daughter? She would have been younger than—than me."

Another quiet conference with the maid, Mary Beth, and an uncertain image swam up, a slat-thin woman with arms stringy with muscle. Nick had known her somewhat; me, not at all.

"Why are you asking about that?" she asked at last, and I had the start of an answer there.

"What happened to her?"

"She ran off," my mother said too fast and too angrily. "She got herself in trouble and she ran off. Why are you asking about this?"

I was silent, and my mother sighed, sending Mary Beth out of the room. I realized how early it was in St. Paul. The sun wouldn't be up there yet. My mother would be in the parlor, where the phone sat in its little niche in the wall.

"Her mother died the year after," my mother said in a different tone. "She never had a father. It's her cousin who teaches school here, and it's some work he's done to be better than what he came from."

"So I'm just meant to forget about it?"

"Everyone else has."

I wondered. The rivers of the world have long memories, and some of the things that live in the Loire and the Seine had been dead for a long time, staring up through the water with their children cradled in their arms.

"I haven't." At least, not after I was reminded.

"What good does it do to remember something like that? Who will forgive you? What price could possibly be paid?"

She sounded tired. Another memory rose up, her niece, my cousin, who stayed with us for a few nights one summer. There had been hushed talks behind closed doors, and a seventeen-year-old girl crying as quietly as she could in the attic room. They'd sent her somewhere, and for a year, she didn't exist, not to the Carraways or the Fays or the Hennesseys or the Wrights, anyone else who mattered. She came back after a year, but she wasn't the same girl who had gone. She smiled and walked with her back straight, no flinching from sudden noises, no running away to hide in her room when the parties got too loud. She was also shorter than she'd been by a good three inches, and how they'd done it, I never knew.

Back in 1922, one hazy July night, I told Jordan about the memory of my cousin. We sat perilously on the balcony railing at her aunt's flat, the stars swimming dreamily above us, the city below.

"She might have done it to herself," Jordan said. "Sometimes, you have to be someone different if you want to survive at all."

Daphne Blackwood couldn't make that change or wouldn't, and I pressed my hand hard over my eyes.

"Is that all you wanted?" my mother said into the silence. I realized it was the longest conversation we had ever had.

"You've never called me by my name."

"Because that's not *your* name, is it?" she asked sharply. "At best, it was left in your care, and you just happened to keep it when the original owner failed to come pick it up."

It was the most she had ever acknowledged my origins or her son's death, and she surprised me again by continuing.

"It's not yours, and if it will give you any comfort, neither is this."

"And if it's not mine, then it's not yours either. Tell me, what would you have done if he had come back after all, if that accident had never happened?"

A long careful breath in the quiet parlor. If I concentrated, scraped the back of my head where the memories were more words than images, I could imagine it, the dark wood, the wool rug, the tassels hanging off the ottoman that had been half-eaten by my mother's spaniel. I had never been in that room. I barely knew the woman.

Then she set the phone down in its cradle, and the distance between St. Paul and New York crackled like thorns.

I ended up at my desk, bent over the blotter and, somehow, asleep. I knew that bad dreams could find me anywhere, but going to my bed felt like a defeat of some sort, an acknowledgment that yesterday had ended, and somehow, I didn't want it to, despite everything that had happened.

Well, yes. If yesterday's over, you don't have any excuse left. You have to admit that I'm gone, and that the voice in your head, well, that's just you, isn't it, old sport? It's only you, and it has only ever been you, talking to yourself and hoping for even an echo from someone else. You would settle for an echo, wouldn't you?

"Wouldn't you?" I retorted, because he had loved his own reflection as few men I have ever met did, even the ones who were vainer by far. Sometimes it felt that if he only stared long enough in the mirror, he would figure it all out, what part of him might be removed, what feature, what memory, might be sheared off to make him what he was meant to be. I had wondered what he might have given for someone to tell him how to truly be himself, because the real version of him wasn't the one in the mirror. It was the one he chased after, harder, I thought, than he had ever run after Daisy Fay.

I slept at my desk as if it was some sort of penance, but then, inevitably, I awoke and it was with March's voice in my head, and that of the anatomical beauty below the hospital.

We don't do anything for free, but they were wrong, one of them had, only perhaps he wasn't one of them at all.

When that thought occurred another came with it, that I had staggered some eight blocks in the middle of the afternoon splattered with blood. New Yorkers were famous for minding their own business, but for that much blood, for red that ran down my shower drain and stained the tub, someone should have screamed or cried out. Instead I had made my way home like a lost lamb, and if I went down the front of the building, I might still find my own bloody fingerprints on the door handle. There are so very few things you can truly walk away from, but it seemed that I had done exactly that.

My hands were shaking, and I had to get air. I threw the window open, and then after a moment, I clambered out onto the fire escape, the rusted black metal freezing and biting into my hands and my knees until I stood. There's no such thing as silence in the city, but the falling snow, thicker now, cushioned the hard edges, pillowed the roar of the cars and the people until I might have been alone.

"Of course I'm not alone," I said to the snow. "That was one of *his* tricks."

When I was a young man, I made the trip between West Egg and Manhattan, and on the way there was a billboard for some optometrist, eyes large and staring as if there was anything to see in the ash yards. Still they saw, and Gatsby told me one terrible night how he had closed them, old magic learned from his Choctaw mother and his cousins, playing chase and tag and least in sight in the fields of North Dakota.

It sounded fantastical to me, a relic of the pioneer days, but, no, he had said, it was still there and so were they, for all that he had left them behind and would not claim them. Their magic was his, and he had used it to save Daisy Fay, shielding her from the death of Myrtle Wilson and the death that came after, and then he had died.

A devil might have slit Hennessey's throat just to see me splattered with blood and arrested for murder, but no devil would hide it.

"Please," I might have said to the winter. My blood roared in my ears.

Gatsby could. Gatsby had.

I turned so quickly that the fire escape creaked. It had been clinging to the building like a grapevine since I had moved in eight years ago, and I had a vision of it choosing this moment, only this moment, to peel away from the brick and smash me to the alley below.

Then I was through the window, shoving on my shoes and grabbing up my coat, and I slammed the door behind me as I ran out into the winter.

C H A P T E R

SEVEN

I ran back to the automat, more crowded now than it had been the day before. I pounded on the panels until an angry man came out from behind the cabinets, and I asked him if anyone had seen a devil the day before, one with his throat cut or another man, shorter than me with close-cropped dark hair, dressed well.

He had no idea who I was talking about, telling me that the point of an automat was not for him to be out front, and that I should be on my way immediately if not sooner. No, he had not heard of anything strange happening the day before.

I left, and I went to the alley, going around behind the dumpster to where Hennessey had shoved me against the wall. The new snow covered the old, and then the kitchen crew's comings and goings obscured the rest. If some of the snow trampled beneath was stained with blood, I could not see it now. For all I knew, Ross Hennessey had been eaten in two bites, and I remembered the anatomical beauty's bright eyes as she told me there was no resurrection from the upper intestine. Good.

From there I went to the Gates, which was closed and no amount of shaking the bars would allow me entry or even bring someone out to shut me up. This wasn't unusual, the Gates closed and opened at strange times, but it sent a panic rabbiting up my spine to sit at the base of my skull, worrying and gnawing until it was hard to get my breath. I caught up against a newspaper box to steady myself, one selling the *Herald Tribune,* and I realized I had written nothing at all for my next column that day. On the front, I could see an article about a murder in Astoria, and I caught the name Ormwell. I fed a dime into the machine, and I read just enough to see that it wasn't Martha Ormwell who had died with two bullets in her heart, but her husband, Francis Skye Ormwell.

The police had his two brothers in custody, and the butler as well, but loving wife Martha they had released this morning. She had been dancing at the Dagger and Garter at the time of the murder, and someone, maybe Gatsby, maybe March, laughed in my head. It was getting crowded in there, and I dropped the paper into the snow and kept on going.

I caught a taxi to Queens General, and this time, no matter how long I walked, the ferns stayed ferns, and there was no office where an anatomical beauty waited and no woman in the ceiling. Instead my hurry and my desperation made me so obvious that I was escorted to the doors, and I was lucky that they didn't call the police on me.

By then I had been tramping in the snow for hours, in and out of buildings and along streets that were barely shoveled. The city was being buried, I saw, the snow falling faster than anyone could move it, and with the sky growing darker by the moment, sooner rather than later the city would give up and let it fall.

I went over to Prospect Park in Brooklyn, timing it poorly enough that there was virtually no one there. The men who came after work had gone, and the ones who came after their wives and children were in bed were still at home, finishing dinner. I walked the paths by the water and under the arch until it was dark, and when a shadow detached itself from under the plane trees, I waited only to see that it was not who I was searching for before I shook my head and walked on.

Nothing had changed, but there was an emptiness to the city that I was certain I had never felt before. If I focused, if I glanced in the diner windows or into the cars, I could make out distinct faces, other people going about their lives just as I had been going about mine. The moment I took my exact gaze off of them, however, they faded into a misty obscurity, as if that sharp image had only been an illusion, and I was alone after all.

I went back to the Gates, but they were still locked against me. I thought someone might be there by now, but even when I banged again on the bars in helpless desperation, no one came out to send me away.

I could wait here, I thought dazedly. *Outside the Gates. Until he came out. Until he came for me.*

I heard what I was thinking, and I shook my head hard. The snow was piling up, and I knew how welcoming snow could be until the moment it wasn't, when it turned cloying and heavy and deadly. My wounded hand was bleeding sluggishly through the filthy bandage. With more than enough backwards looks to turn me to salt, I started on my way home.

I could have called for a cab, but instead I walked the whole way back, and in every alleyway and every doorway, I expected him to step out, to call my name, to smile and—

What?

I didn't know what came after that, but I knew that the worst had happened some twenty years ago, and now I had to know what came next.

I managed to return to my apartment without being run down in the street or knocked into the river, but when the door closed behind me, I was trapped. I paced the confines of the apartment that I had turned into a refuge from the world, and now I could only see it as a cage—warm, comfortable, mine like no other place was, but a cage nonetheless.

I ate something and didn't taste it, I lay down on the sofa and couldn't sleep, and I sat out on the fire escape until I so disturbed a woman across the alley that she stuck her head out to scream at me to go in.

Finally, I called the operator, and I ignored her slightly scandalized tone at my calling Paris at this hour. I hung up, paced some more. There was no room for anything in me but a need to be out searching. If you don't search, you don't find, and abruptly I could not take not finding. I could not bear it.

Something was hanging over me. I could feel it now, cathedral arches that I was only now realizing were the legs of some great spider. Somewhere above, something was looking at me, eyes picking up any ambient shine to better see me, to track my movements, to see which way I might run when the walls closed in. Then it would swoop down from above, jaws open and—

No, not from above, I thought, almost giddy. *From below.*

I liked that just as well, and then the phone rang, the operator prim as if it wasn't her business what I got up to with Paris.

"Nick. What."

"It's him. It's him. She—they told me it couldn't be, that he had been *eaten,* and—"

With remarkable patience, Jordan let me get the whole thing out, and I was wound so very tightly I ended up telling her everything, all of it, from Queens General to Hennessey to my frantic search today.

When I finally came to a stop, more to catch my breath than for any other reason, she was silent on the other side of the world. The only thing that told me she hadn't gone to sleep was her breathing, light and quick. She snored when she was genuinely asleep, something she didn't know to fake or felt was too crude to do even if it might have made her artifice better.

"All right," she said finally. "So?"

"So? Jordan, listen—"

"I have been. I listened a few days ago, and I listened now, and what has changed? So Gatsby is back, or maybe he's not, or maybe it is him, or maybe it's not. Who cares?"

I sputtered something indignant, and she laughed, a bright, brittle sound. She had never had any patience for Gatsby. I thought she might have been one of the only people in the city who wasn't at least a little afraid of him, and that didn't make her like him any better.

"Not me," she said. "I certainly don't care. He's where he belongs—"

"Jordan!"

"No one put a gun to his head to make the deals he did, and anyway, you wrote your ever so clever book to tell the whole world what that deal was about, didn't you? His house was Hell's favorite way station, and when I think of who came and went, who *disappeared*—"

"I don't recall you caring much when you went that summer."

"Of course I didn't," she said coldly. "I couldn't stand most of the people I saw there, and some of them are better off disappeared than troubling the people I actually liked. Some of those people are right where they belong, and I won't lose sleep over it. It doesn't matter what I lose sleep over. What matters is that Gatsby made deals with Hell, and like everyone else who has, he lost. You know that, right?"

I grimaced. I had called her to clear my head. I didn't like what I was seeing now that I was clearer.

"He's where he belongs, or he isn't, and one thing that I thought writing your little book would have told you is that it has nothing to do with you. Do you understand that? It has nothing at all to do with you, and it never has. Or me. So I do not know why we're talking about it now."

"Because he's back," I insisted, and I heard her breathe, two long exhales as she sought enough patience not to shout at me.

"And what are you going to do about it?"

"I need to find him. I need to talk with him."

"Oh, are you going to apologize for writing him up as the playboy of the western world? Because I am still waiting for your apology, if you're taking requests."

"I didn't write your story, I wrote mine."

"Of course you did. All right, if you can tell me why you want to see him, and if you can convince me that it's the truth, I'll tell you how to do it."

The thing was, I believed her. Jordan always had a way of existing harder than everyone else around her, even when she was sitting in the corner and watching everyone make fools of themselves. If she said she knew how to find him, she did, and I would no more doubt her now than when she was taking me to the illegal gin joints in Harlem and the Bronx.

"Of course I have to find him," I said stiffly. "Otherwise, what is it all for?"

"You got a novel, and, from what Patsy tells me, a very nice advance out of it. I should think that would be plenty for most normal people. Why don't you try again?"

"I have to find out how the story ends."

"You of all people know that the story ends when you say it does, whenever you want it to. The story ended in the summer of 1922. The story ended when we said goodbye that fall. The story could end right now, if you wanted it to. One more try, Nick, and then I have to go back to packing."

"Packing?" I asked, stalling. "Where are you going?"

"London first. And then Helsinki, where Tove has said I may have the rear bedroom until this all blows over. It's funny, you know. All this time, and I'm staying in other people's bedrooms again, in other people's houses and other people's countries. I had thought that maybe Paris would take."

More quietly, "I can hear the guns, you know. And I hear the dead men too. Every night, they walk up and down the street. This place is haunted, Nick."

I swallowed hard.

"It was when I was there too. It's good that you're going. And if you want to come back to New York—"

"I won't."

"But if you do, I'll be here. Whatever you need."

"It won't be you," she said, but maybe she smiled a little when she said it. "All right. Come on. Once more. Why do you need to see Jay Gatsby so damned much?"

For a moment, I thought I still couldn't say it, but then I shrugged because he was in my ear, saying it was just words, old sport, nothing but words, and we were greater than words, and he always had been.

"Because who would I be if I didn't?"

I heard her breath on the other end of the line, soft, almost wounded, which was wrong. I was years past being able to hurt Jordan, and when she came back on the line, her voice was clear and firm.

"You could be anyone you damned well liked, you sorry excuse for—" She huffed in exasperation. "But all right. I have to figure out how to get my maid, my cook, and my entire wardrobe across the channel, so I'll let you have this one."

She paused, because Jordan had always liked to make sure people were listening before she spoke. If she hadn't been foreign and a woman, she would have made a very good politician.

"Given that you have been up to your neck in infernal waters all week, it's frankly embarrassing you have not come up with this yourself. Devils are always willing to talk to you, aren't they, so long as you've got something they're interested in?"

I rubbed my chest over my heart.

"Do I—?"

"Oh, who knows. I barely know if I've got one. At least, no devil has ever come running after me with stars in their eyes."

"Thank you, Jordan. I suppose I hadn't thought that was a bargain I could make."

"Or you didn't want to, because you were afraid you would if you could."

There was a sudden noise on her end of the line, a great splintering sound followed by a boom. For a moment, I thought we had been cut off, but then she was there again. I imagined her going pale, her hand tight around the telephone, but her chin lifted as perfectly as if she were balancing her dignity there.

"Oh dear, it sounds as if I really must go, but Nick, one more thing? Don't sleep with the dead. You're not one of them, after all."

I gave her the last word, because I loved her too, and then there was nothing but static on the line. I wondered in a vague way where the connection stopped when it was cut off like that. Did the signal travel all the way to Paris to stop short of Jordan's flat on the Left Bank, or was it cut off directly in the center between us, somewhere in the middle of the Atlantic Ocean? Maybe it ended just after it left my home, over and done with before it started. I set the phone gently on its cradle, and I sat back in my chair, waiting for morning.

Dawn, when it came, slid slowly and cautiously from night. The snow had not stopped, and I looked out into the street to see the cars half-buried, tracks made in the white by the people who already had to be at their jobs. The swagged clouds hung low over our heads, forbidding any thought of the sun or of summer, and I called the operator again.

"I'd like to be put through to the Gates by Columbia Street," I said, as if I were doing something normal, and the operator rang back with their answering service, where the phone was picked up by someone who sounded like a brisk young man at any law firm or advertising company.

"I'd like to leave a message for a devil with a cut throat," I said. "I'm afraid I do not know his name."

"Of course, sir. It's all right, I know who you are thinking of. What message do you have for him?"

"I have for sale an item that would very much interest him."

"Of course. And who should I say has called?"

"Nicholas Carraway, and I can be reached at this number."

There was a brief pause.

"Nicholas Carraway, the author?"

No, I wanted to say. *Absolutely not.*

"I've written a few things, yes."

"I liked your latest," he said, almost shyly. "We all did."

"I'm so pleased," I said automatically, and he laughed at that.

"You probably ought not be, given. But I won't keep you. He will call you back."

I hung up the phone, and finally, I could take off my shoes and go lie down on my bed. I felt as if I had passed a good decade in the last few days, and when I closed my eyes, I heard more voices than Gatsby's in my head. There was the anatomical beauty's, asking if my heart was breaking. There was Jordan's, cool and amused even under fire, and the voice of the man I had met the night after Christmas, warm and shy and oddly gentle in a way that I would remember for a while.

Somewhere beneath it, I reached for the voice of Daphne Blackwood, trying to find her in the bare words that were all I had of that night, but there was nothing. I couldn't even find his voice, which, after all, I used every day. If it was mine, then so was she, and if it wasn't, then I didn't know what came next.

I put my pillow over my face, and when I slept, I had dreams that I forgot upon waking, knowing only that I was grateful that I forgot.

When I woke, the light was stronger, but the snow was still falling. It did not look as if it would stop, and I was just rising from my bed when the phone rang.

"Call for Mr. Carraway from the Gates."

"This is Mr. Carraway speaking. Please put it through."

There was a buzz, and then a click, and the voice that came through was a dull knock on a pineboard coffin.

"Hello, Mr. Carraway. You called and said that you had something I would be interested in."

"I believe I do, yes."

"Well?"

"I'm afraid it is nothing I care to discuss over the phone. I would like to meet."

There was a faint sound of amusement. I imagined air hissing past the torn flesh of his throat, ruffling the shreds of skin, the severed windpipe.

"Don't you all. All right. The Gates are open—"

"No, not the Gates."

"Where, then?"

I swallowed, my hand going to my own throat, which was currently whole. The idea had been in my head ever since I woke up.

"August 7th. Do you—?"

"Sentimental thing," he said with a smile in his voice. "All right. I know it. Shall we say this afternoon? It will only be worse out tonight."

I remembered with surprise that it was New Year's Eve. Now that I listened for it, I could hear shouting in the alley, and honking as well, as people poured into their cars and took to the snowy streets.

We agreed on two, and when we hung up, I could feel my heart thrumming in my chest. Once, long ago, Jordan had taken out what was there before and given me something new. A new heart hadn't freed me—that kind of surgery only gives you time unless you are willing to free yourself, and I had never wanted to. Even now, I still didn't know if I did.

C H A P T E R

EIGHT

August 7th was located in Gowanus, on the top floor of one of the warehouses there. On bad days, the wind from over the water bore a chemical reek, and even on good days there was something tired about the neighborhood, worn thin and strange. Despite that, it was one of the places in the city where you saw more salamandrinas and candles than Edison bulbs. There was meant to be a whole colony of imps down there, abandoned when New York put the ban into effect. Some of their owners had them installed in their homes up in the Hamptons or bequeathed them to eager young relatives in Chicago or San Francisco. More, it seemed like, let them loose by the river and against all expectation, they had survived to breed, living in the dark corners under the docks and the warehouse rafters.

As I made my way to August 7th, I could hear them in the shadows, the restless clattering of their claws and the chimes of old broken chains around their throats. I remembered one morning while I was seeing Jordan, a lifetime ago. I woke up in the guest room wearing borrowed pajamas with Jordan napping on top of the covers beside me and an imp at the foot of the bed. It didn't belong to her great-aunt, who didn't care for them. It must have belonged to one of Mrs. Howard's suffragette friends, who stayed as late as I did, and later. That imp wore a diamond collar, and it stared at me with an avid kind of curiosity tilting its barbed head.

"What kind of thing are you?" it had hissed gently.

Its mistress called it away before I had to admit that I didn't know. Twenty years older and likely about to do something profoundly stupid, I knew a little more. I wasn't the real Nick Carraway, but real mattered less than I had thought it did. I could imagine Jordan huffing a long exasperated breath, *What's so important about real anyway?*

There was a teenage girl perched just inside the double doors at August 7th, slouched over a podium stacked with menus. She wore a braided wool blanket over her shoulders against the chill, and she looked up at the bell when I entered, wiping the sleep from her eyes.

"Lunch, sir?"

"Yes, if you please. And a private room as well, if you have one to spare."

Her lips quirked, acknowledging my polite fiction. Of course they had a room to spare—the place had never been all that popular.

She took up a menu and shrugged off the blanket, revealing the long dark uniform that called back to house servants from the turn of the century.

"Right this way," she said.

She opened the door and led me into summer.

The light was pure and bright, gold with the kind of weight that settled warmly on your shoulders and your bare head. That was the biggest difference, and perhaps the most important one. The tall windows, which from the outside were boarded up, looked over a river valley in late summer, and one of them was thrown open to let in a fresh wind from the water, carrying with it the smell of leaves and grass and something slightly metallic beneath it.

There was a deed of sale just by the door, committing the

possession of August 7, 1922 in the town of Scarlett to L. R. Kilkenney. It was signed and notarized, the signature of the mayor small and cramped, Kilkenney's a broad flourish. Kilkenney had paid eighty dollars for the day, and he had made good use of it since. In 1930, he'd opened up this place, a bit of hoarded time wedged between the warehouses and the docks. It was a marvel, but a common sort of thing, and mostly forgotten in the age of iron radiators and air conditioning. It was considered quaint and a little silly, and I was stepping into the past in more ways than one.

The room the girl took me to was small but well-appointed. There was a table with three chairs, and the bench at the bay window was scattered with round cushions. A small desk held some fresh stationery and a phone that would ring the front of the house, and the girl set her menus down on the table.

"There's a man with a cut throat coming after me," I told her. "If you could bring us a bottle of demoniac when he comes, that would be perfect."

She gave me another amused look, an antique asking for an antique, from her point of view, probably, and I stood at the bay window, looking out over the Scarr River. Coming in from New York in winter, it was easy to see this place as a moment out of time, to appreciate the slight sense of disorientation and the strange longing at the center of my chest as the heartbreak it truly was. That's a promise you hear more and more, that of course things can return to what they were before—and if you live long enough, you eventually realize that mostly, it's a lie.

I turned as the door opened behind me and the cut-throat devil entered, removing his hat politely, and with a hastily wiped bottle in his hands.

"Impolite," he said, holding it up.

"But you'll bear it, won't you? Because I asked for it."

He smiled a little wider at that, and he set the bottle on the table to remove his coat. He moved easily from task to task, as if one thing mattered as little as any other. It must have been how he slit Hennessey's throat, with that same grace and perhaps even that same small smile on his face.

He looked nothing like Gatsby—in fact, he looked more like me. No one would take us for relatives, but he was also tall and dark-haired, though with more weight than I carried. He looked like no one in particular, for which I was grateful, and if he only wore a scarf, he would be unremarkable until the blood at his throat wet it through. He must have caught me looking, for he pointed at his throat.

"Does it bother you?"

"Would you cover it up if I said yes?"

"You could ask me," he said, almost flirtatiously, and I shook my head.

"No, thank you. And it doesn't bother me. I have seen worse."

"I'm sure you have. I read your book, you know."

"Everyone has, it seems."

"Not that one, though I heard it was a laugh. No, the first one. The one about Paris, after."

I tried not to be too flattered, but no one had read that one. It had been reviewed dispassionately, it had sold indifferently, and I still had two dozen copies stashed in the closet at home.

"I hope you enjoyed it," I said, and he sat at the table, gesturing for me to take a seat.

"I liked it very much," he said, uncorking the bottle. "I was in the war too, you know."

"I hadn't thought Hell sent any troops."

"Oh, of course it didn't. But I remember Montenegro, and the Cemi River. On a clear night in June, we looked out over the fords, and we saw women in the rapids. They were enormous, as long as the Paris guns, swimming just under the water with their naked sides silvered by the moon, and their eyes were like wells as they glanced at us on their way by—"

I took a breath and did not push back from the table. The last time I had heard that story I was twenty years younger and naked in bed, his hand touching my hair.

"Unkind," I said, and he tilted his head, still smiling, but cold.

"Of course I am. I am also here because you asked for me, aren't I?"

He poured me a generous portion of demoniac, but I nodded at his glass.

"You as well. I don't care to drink alone."

I thought for a moment he wouldn't. I had never seen a devil drink that stuff. They said it was brewed out of their blood, but they said many things. He only shrugged slightly and poured himself a measure as well.

In the thick-sided tumblers, the demoniac had a velvety purple hue, nearly black, and it threw back light in a strange way. When I picked up my glass, I could smell something heavy and sweet and dry, and underneath it, something rotten. If it was blood, anyone's blood, it had gone bad.

"What should I call you?" I asked, taking a sip. It had a piney bite to it, dry and with a sweet and unpleasant finish. It evaporated off my tongue to go straight to my head, and I didn't look at the things that started to crawl at the edges of my vision. The devil drank as well, licking his teeth with a sour face before he set it down again.

"I take it you wouldn't appreciate calling me Jay, or the face I could put on for you."

"No. Not in the slightest."

"All right. You knew March. You can call me December."

"Knew?"

"Disappointing performance, whining excuses. Gone the way of all teeth. We had him yesterday at the Gates. Was that you pounding on the door? We were rather occupied."

December smiled wider, or no, not smiled, though it was easy to think he did. He bared his teeth and reminded me that we were all eaters.

"I'm sorry to hear that."

"So polite. So I am December, and you, you don't even have a name, do you? Not a real one of your own. Is that something you would like, a name of your own?"

"I can have any name I want if I go in front of a judge," I said evenly.

"I would give you a real one," December said. "It would belong to you until the day you died, all yours and one you didn't inherit from a rapist. That would be a nice thing to have, and I would give you a new face as well, one that was properly your own. I have some to spare, and then you could be anyone you like."

"I can already be anyone I like. All it would take is walking away from what I have now. It's all still mine, even if the face and name aren't."

"But it's not enough, is it?" he asked, and it probably said something that he didn't even bother with sincerity.

"No." I took another sip from the glass in front of me, and to show willing, he did as well. "I suppose that's what you trade in, the not enough."

"If you say so—"

"Why did you cut Ross Hennessey's throat?"

For a moment, there was something real on his face, real and inhuman perhaps, but real.

"Because I wanted to."

"Of course. Thank you for telling me."

He pushed away from the table, pacing to the bay window. I picked up his drink and mine and followed him, and when I pressed the glass into his hand, he took it from me.

"You're standing very close," December observed. "Are you interested in something simpler?"

I was grateful when he had enough taste not change his face, and I only examined him up and down.

How small you are, the thought occurred. *How little you matter, how little you mean compared to—*

He could be handsome if you chose to see him as such, but I shook my head, and he made a sound like the threat of a motor under strain.

"You shouldn't waste my time if you know what's good for you. You see, the thing about time, dear heart, is that once it's gone, you can't get it back."

I nodded to the window where a beautiful summer day in 1922 shaded towards the long slow evening. I smiled a little and leaned closer.

"I think you can," I said. "Of course you can get it back, if only you fought hard enough to do so. Even you."

"Even me," he scoffed, but I could tell that something had caught him, either a memory of the past or the possibility of a future.

I drank, and so did he.

"Tell me what you want," he said at last. "Even you aren't lonely enough that you would dangle your soul in front of something like me for conversation."

"I might be. No one talks to me these days, not really."

"They're too afraid that you'll write a book about them. I heard that Pamela Buchanan was seeking legal action against you."

"People say many things. But I do want to talk. I don't mind if it has a price."

He sharpened at that, and I wasn't sure whether it was his own doing or whether it was the demoniac I had drunk doing it for me. It was strange stuff. It gave you visions. It showed you the world under the world, or the world the way it could be or the world you most wanted or the world you least wanted. It had been very popular during Prohibition, but it was harder to get now. Mostly people preferred cocaine.

"Now you are marginally more interesting. Give me your soul, and I'll talk as long as you like."

"And about whatever I like?"

"Yes. It may not be the truth, however. That costs more than you're worth."

"I'm a writer, I have no business with the truth," I said cheerfully. "And you'll get my soul when I am satisfied. Are we agreed?"

He hesitated, looking over the bargain from end to end, and at last he shrugged.

"It's your soul. Yes."

"Let's drink to it."

We did, and the demoniac this time was thicker than it was a moment before. It brought a fevered blush to my cheeks, and December loosened his tie, sitting at the bay window and looking down over the Scarr River.

"What a place you have up here," he whispered.

"Tell me about North Dakota," I said, and he glared at me.

"Ben Harrison made it a state in 1889, the capital is Bismarck—"

"No, tell me what you remember about it."

December smirked.

"Should I put on his face?"

"Not yet, no."

He leaned back in the bay window, more confident now, even a little coquettish. He hitched one foot up on the edge of the seat, clasping both hands easily around his knee. It was designed to be charming—it looked familiar.

"All right. I've never been to Bismarck. I was born north of Van Hook Arm, and Bismarck might as well have been the moon back then. The sky was the only thing in the world that wasn't dirt or trash pine, and if you stared up at it, you might fall in and be lost forever. My mother told me that, that that was what happened to her mother and father, and they left her behind to fend for herself."

"Your mother. You told me once she was Choctaw."

"I did, she was—she was—"

He scowled, running a finger along the split flesh at his throat like a lady might finger a locket.

"I don't want to talk about her," he said, standing away from the window, and that was what he had said then too.

"That's fine. Tell me about Dan Cody."

"What's to tell? Healthy old bastard with money. He saw me, he liked me, and off we went to see the world. Then his bitch of an ex-wife decided to push me out of the inheritance I had earned rolling him out of his own sick four nights out of the week and telling him how tough and smart he was the other three."

He gave me a defiant look as if daring me to question him, but I only nodded thoughtfully.

"You never liked him much, did you?"

"I liked him well enough. I don't like anyone much. *You* know that."

"No. You just love them."

He looked down at that, tugging at his cut throat almost modestly.

"You're the only one who ever believed that."

"I wrote a book about it, as a matter of fact."

December jumped as if remembering himself. He turned away from the window, walking to the desk to pick up the phone and then put it back down again. There was nothing in the room but the two of us, and he poured himself some more demoniac. I took some as well, and it was kinder going down this time, as if it had decided that I was a friend.

"Is this what gets it hard for you?" December asked cruelly. "Teenage boys on long ocean voyages with dissolute old men?"

"Tell me about the first time you met Daisy, then."

"Fireworks," he said flatly, guarded now. "The whole of Chicago lit up with electricity for the first time at the World's Fair. Blood and gold and the possibility of it all being mine."

"You don't want to talk about Daisy. That's fine. Talk about Jordan instead. You know, I still speak with her sometimes. She's angry about the book."

He snorted, more human about the woman he didn't care about than the one he did. His impatience made him easier in his skin, and he tapped his fingers on the glass in a gesture that hurt with its familiarity.

"She's angry? When she was always following along after Daisy and desperate to be in the society pages? Please. That one would be slitting throats on the Shanghai docks if she hadn't been stolen into money, and she knows it. Everyone liked her, though. It's easy to like her when you don't really know her. I could see why you were so gone on her."

"I was gone on you too."

He didn't even blink at that, instead laughing and sitting down at the table. I took my place across from him, and it was one more evening in West Egg in 1922, him talking, me adoring, and it didn't matter that I was twenty years older and he was dead in every way that mattered. It was real then, and it was real now.

"Really, Nick. It's nice of you to say so, but you've always been a little too free with it, haven't you. Your heart, I mean. Did you ever learn any better?"

"I think so. And your heart. What have you learned about it?"

"That I never needed it! I never needed it at all, and I would have ended better if I never listened to the ridiculous things it said."

He shook his head at a younger man's foolishness

"Which of us did you think had the better of it?" he asked earnestly. "A heart of paper or a heart made from hungry gears. Would you trade?"

"If you asked me, maybe. That day I was talking to March, you came after me. Why?"

"Because I needed to talk to you. You've got something I want. Do you know what it is yet?"

I nodded, and he smiled, bright as the sun glinting over an old clean river. They'd built paper mills along the Scarr River, and it would never again be what it was here, bought and stolen away.

"Well, then."

"You always liked talking about yourself. I did too. Tell me how you found out about me back then. I can't imagine I took the cottage next to your palace by accident."

"Did you ever think you had? Of course you didn't. I went looking for loose ends, that's all. You know Daisy's people, and Tom's, they were all stitched up so tight. I needed someone who had been cut loose, someone alone. You people are all so very vulnerable when you are alone."

I was silent, but he leaned over to set his hand on mine. I had changed the bandage, and it was as white as snow under his fingers, his nails black as midnight. He was warmer than I was, and he ran the edge of his thumbnail over the gauze bandage. He wasn't particularly gentle, and a low twinge of pain ran up my arm.

"I'm good at being alone," he said quietly. "I never should have stopped."

"I'm glad you did. I was always glad of you."

"Foolish," he said, but he turned my hand to expose my wrist, thoughtful even if he wasn't precisely thinking of me. He brought my hand to his mouth, and I saw how sharp his teeth really were, but then he only kissed the skin there, no pain at all.

"That night in Prospect Park," I said, because December could never have kissed me like that. "Tell me why you helped me."

"Because I missed you."

I meant to let it stand, and I found a shred of pride because I couldn't. Instead, I jerked my hand away from his, turning away. I almost went straight out of the room because to hell with all of this, except that that wasn't the kind of lie that December would have told.

"To hell with you," I said, going to the window, and he rose to follow.

"I do, of course I do, I missed you."

"Liar again. You missed New York. You missed the world on

a string, you missed being the mysterious man with the mansion on West Egg, the biggest story anyone could ever tell."

"And I missed you," he cried, but I wouldn't look at him, and Jay Gatsby could never stand being ignored.

"I missed you, I love you," he insisted, and when I wouldn't turn, he came to lean against my back, resting his chin on my shoulder. This close, I could smell the demoniac on his breath and also the cologne that I was fairly certain he hadn't been wearing before.

"You don't. Tell me why."

"Because I needed you. You know why, don't you? You wrote a whole damned book about it."

"I knew you. And I remember you."

His nails bit into my sides, sharp through the fabric.

"No, I— So go on. Tell me."

"You're Jay Gatsby, born Jimmy Gatz whether you liked it or not, and you didn't. You are ambitious and ferocious and hungry, and if you can get what you want, then to hell with the rest. You're foolish and brilliant and not as smart as you think you are and a complete fucking bastard when things don't go your way."

The man behind me uttered a strangled cry, and then he laughed.

"Yes. I am."

"You're the American Dream, if the American Dream is a broken thing, smashed up on the side of the road and left behind by people in better cars with more secure fortunes. You've killed people, and you've saved them, and each means as little to you as the other because life and death have never interested you. You never cared about salvation and damnation either, or love and hate."

"What did I care about?"

His voice in my ear was low and guttural. His nails dug into my sides. He was shorter than he had been before, and I knew that I should not, for any price, look behind me.

"You care about yourself and the things that you wanted to be a part of you. You wanted money, you wanted fame, you wanted the lie of how you got them better than you wanted any kind of truth. You wanted Daisy or a girl like her, and sometimes, you wanted me.

"You wanted the stars in the sky and you wanted all the gold on Wall Street, and you wanted all eyes on you, and fuck you, Jay, but you fucking got it in the end, didn't you, and all it cost you was—"

"Everything," he purred, and there was a terrible sound behind me, a shriek of tearing metal, the ripping fabric sound of severing skin, a thin scream on too little breath, and I closed my eyes but not before I caught a glimpse of what was happening reflected in the glass in front of me.

It was a mangle of limbs and teeth, a halo of murder and glad hunger, and there was no resurrection from the upper intestine, but this wasn't a resurrection. There wasn't a word for what this was, except that it was wrong. It was wanting that could claw itself back into existence, and if all Jay Gatsby was was wanting, then he would sharpen it into a knife—or perhaps I would—and cut himself through to the world again. I closed my eyes tight until it was quiet, and a hand landed on my shoulder, squeezing gently.

"Oh, don't take on so, old sport. It's over now."

I turned back, and the first thing that struck me was how young he looked. It's funny how at every age you think yourself an adult, mature and wise to the ways of the world, but Jay Gatsby at thirty—he had never gotten any older—looked positively boyish to me, with his close-cropped dark hair and his generous smile and his clothes a little loose on his frame. He was shorter than December was, and lighter as well, and he tugged at his cuffs to give them a better set.

"It's you," I said, and he smiled.

"Yes. I knew you could do it."

I laughed wildly.

"No, you didn't. You only hoped and wanted."

"It has been enough before. Come here and have a seat, you look like you are going to faint."

I carefully did not look at the sloppy pile of bloody skin and rags on the floor. It occurred to me that he had split the difference between himself and December straight off, and I stared at the ceiling for a moment until I could breathe.

"Is it really you?"

"Mostly." He winked at me. "I'm built out of what you remember me to be, but that's no bad thing, is it, to be made from the memories of someone who loved you? I'm as much Jay Gatsby as you are Nick Carraway."

I laughed at that, hopelessly and desperately and heartbroken like I thought I had not been in a long time. As real as each other and as false as well, what a pair we were. He stroked my hand until the fit passed and I could speak again.

"What will you do, now that you are back?"

"I don't know. See the world. Catch up with some old friends. Collect some debts that are due to me."

"You're lying," I said, and his eyes shuttered like a well-pleased cat's, his nails sharper on the back of my hand. His nails and his eyes were as black as midnight.

"Well, twenty years in Hell change a man," he said diplomatically. "It may be that I have a few plans in mind, a few prospects I should check on, now that things up here are getting so interesting."

"I thought you might stay a while—"

Gatsby gave me a patient but unsparing look.

"With you? Now, Nick. Could you imagine me doing so?"

"No."

"Well, then."

He rose from the chair, and I could already see that restless, remorseless quality in him, the urge to be doing, acquiring, conquering. I could have made him anything, and instead I made him what he actually was. Twenty years ago, I might have said I was too honest to do otherwise, but now I suspected a certain species of forlorn and foolish pride instead. If I could not be happy, I would be proud.

"Thank you. No one else could have done it, and I don't believe anyone has ever loved me as well as you do."

I started to say what a prize that was, but he put his hands on either side of my face, holding me still as he leaned down and kissed me. It was teeth and heat, an invasion because he knew no other way to kiss. His tongue pushed into my mouth, and all I could taste was the dry feverish sweetness of demoniac. It was kissing memory and longing and regret, and it made me ache because I had missed him so much.

I seized him by the borrowed jacket, suddenly afraid that he would leave me again. It was a violent gesture—he could not have easily pulled away, but he only laughed. His hand settled lightly over mine, and he took a seat on the table, tugging me up so that I came to stand between his knees. There was something unaccustomed about it, and perhaps I had worked more of my own desire into him than either of us had guessed. He had never kissed me like this, as if it was the only thing that he wanted to be doing. Right now, there was no fortune, no Daisy, no ringing phone, no sword over his head. It was only him, and it was only me, and it was August 7th, 1922.

His mouth on mine grew more insistent, pulling me forward so that my weight pressed him to his back on the table. I stood back a moment to look down at him, my hand braced beside his head, and he reached up to wrap his fingers loosely around my wrist.

"Do you know how often I thought of this in the dark?"

"You didn't."

"You must allow yourself to be surprised sometimes, Nick. Cynicism is so very dull."

It was hard, so hard, to do as he said, to allow myself to be surprised. I am a cynic, after all, and I could guess at his motive for all manner of things, for kissing me as if he were dying for it, for pressing his thigh up between my legs. I could imagine how much he'd missed having a proper body of his own. He laughed quietly, kissing my ear. He kissed my mouth until it was sore, taking his time, casually digging his nails into my sides. He didn't need Hell to make him cruel—he always had been, in all the ways that I liked.

"You still think too much," he said warmly. "You're just the same."

I wasn't, of *course* I wasn't, but I forgot that too because suddenly I smelled his cologne, L'Ambre de Carthage with its heart of olivewood and notes of amber and tea. No one wore that any longer, too rich, too *much,* but of course he did, and I buried my face in his throat.

"I want. I want—"

"Easy," but he laughed as he said it, and it reminded me that he loved easy things. He loved it when things fell into his open hands before he knew he wanted them, when things went down for him because he smiled, when everything could be had, not even for the asking but because of who and what he was.

If I had made him, I wanted to see that I had crafted well, and agreeably, he allowed me to examine him from the skin out. I found the scattering of small moles along his ribs. On the inside of his right knee, there was the scar from a fall in the woods from when he was a boy. I had given him all his teeth, though—the man I knew was missing the rearmost molar on the right side of his jaw and when I put my tongue back there to feel, he was so whole I thought for a moment that I must be kissing someone else.

His patience for my explorations ran out quickly, and he rose to put me with my back to the door, one hand coming to turn the latch before undoing my trousers with a kind of military efficiency. He should have been in uniform with a cigarette in his mouth, and he glanced up at me slyly as if he could imagine which way my thoughts ran. Gunshots and the threat of mustard gas forgave as much as his parties did, and sometimes, I missed the excuse that I might die tomorrow.

"Stop that," he said, warm hand clasped around my cock. "I don't want you thinking of that just now. Think of me instead."

I did, just him, only him, and even when I wanted to keep my eyes open, they finally shut against what he was doing to me, how good it felt. It would be romantic to say it was better than any I'd had since him or before, but it wasn't. Instead it was the best because it was him, and he was always bigger than romance or tragedy. He was himself, a defiance of definition or comparison.

I went down on my knees, clumsy in this as I had always been, and he smiled at the memory, his hand in my hair, the tip of his thumb sliding along my lips to part them. In someone else, it would be an invitation to suck or to gag, but instead, he pressed the ball of his thumb along my lower canines before turning his hands to test the upper ones as well.

"What a fine bite you have," and I did. I'd leave bruises if I was allowed.

"Darling thing," he said, as he had said so many times, and it hit me in the chest even as I leaned in to take him. The wrongness of it sent a deep shudder through my body that he mistook for desire. Perhaps there are some things you can only see kneeling and hungry for what someone might give you, and I saw him better then, the reality of Gatsby as he had been and the reality of the one before me now. He was used to me wanting, and for most of my life, I had thought he was like me in that regard, both of us nothing but want—but where the wanting might be its own satisfaction for me, his was like those flames he had called up in the alley, a blazing emptiness forever feeding on itself.

This man said the same things, how sweet I was, how much he loved me, but I had never mistaken his desire for love then, and I had made him real enough that I could not do it now. If he was real, he wouldn't have loved me. If he loved me, he wouldn't be real.

I wanted him to love me. I wanted him to be real. I had thought I would have to choose one or the other, but now I understood, finally, that I couldn't have either because I would always want both.

Still it was good, and I wanted him, and maybe I liked being taken advantage of by someone some part of me still insisted was worth it. It was worth it, all of it, his hand in my hair, the sounds he made, how he felt, how he looked. He was and wasn't the man I had known, and it didn't matter because we wouldn't exist outside of this room. The words on a page are no less real after the fire has consumed them. Being with him was the absence from myself that I wanted most.

Except for one, however, no absence from yourself is ever final, and eventually, I stumbled to the chair and began setting myself to rights. He did the same, watching me with an avid satisfaction that embarrassed me more than the act itself, and I watched as he went to the phone, calling the front desk and speaking quietly to the girl there. Then he hung up and came back to me.

We broke apart when there was a discreet knock at the door, and he didn't bother straightening his clothes before he went to answer it. I started to warn him that things were stricter now, nowhere near as easy as they used to be when last he was around, but he had never been willing to take a warning.

He spoke briefly and kindly with the girl at the door, and she returned with the things he'd asked for. He closed the door, latching it again, and turned to me with a smile.

"I'm bound for Europe on the first ship I can catch, but before I go, Nicholas, I want to give you a present."

"A present."

"Yes, don't sound so surprised. First, let's have your heart."

"My—"

"Oh, of course you know how. You've always known, haven't you?"

I didn't. I remembered what my grandmother had done. I knew in a dim and cobwebbed part of my brain what Jordan had done, and I caught my breath.

"I can't."

"Of course you can." Gatsby winked. "Just for me. Just like old times, hm?"

Hesitantly, I unbuttoned my shirt, and he handed me a steak knife from the kitchen. It was serrated and sharp, and I thought briefly of the Sheffield razor my great-uncle had used to take his own face off.

It hurt, of course it hurts to take out your own heart. Nothing hurts more unless it's a bullet or mustard gas in your lungs or a car crash or the thousand other things that hurt more. Still I was sweating and crying by the end, and at the last there was a crumpled paper heart in Gatsby's hand and blood all down my front. I couldn't do it as neatly as Jordan could, no matter how talented my great-grandmother was. I might not have been able to do it at all without the demoniac.

Gatsby shook out the paper heart delicately, spreading it out on the table. I could see calendar squares on the damp and crumpled paper, and as well, Gatsby's name written in defiance of the clean start she had tried to give me.

"Did she use her planner to make this? Good grief."

Gatsby shook his head, and with a touch of his fingers, he incinerated it, a magnesium flare that was gone before I was done flinching. He brushed the fine powdery white ash off the table, and then he lay a clean sheet of paper in front of me as well as a pen. He traced a heart over the paper with the tip of his finger, burning away the rest, and then he tapped its center.

"And there you are. We're a few months short of Valentine's Day, but here's one for you."

"A heart."

"Yours, if you want it. Or you might go on without one, but I don't think that's quite your style, is it?"

I took up the fountain pen he set beside the paper. It felt strange and heavy in my hand, just a common Arnold pen with the marbleized cream and black, and I hesitantly put the point to the paper before glancing up at Gatsby.

He was already putting December's hat back on his head, making a face at the fit, but deciding it would do well enough until he could get better. He was good at getting better, always had been. He nodded at me.

"Be a little kind to yourself, please. If you can be whoever you want, wouldn't it be nice to be someone you liked?"

He turned and left, as some part of me always knew he would, and taking a deep breath, I started to write.

I started with the night after Christmas, when I had met a man in front of the statue of the lioness and her cubs at Prospect Park. He had offered me a cigarette, which I had declined, let me kiss him instead, and touch him, and he had touched me in turn, his cold hand sliding up my shirt with a hunger that was somehow polite as well. Prospect Park was a favorite of professional men, but polite ones were rare, and we lingered long after we should have been gone, him retying my tie for me with a joke about my needing a wife at home. He laughed when I mentioned that this was the best Christmas I'd had lately. He had left before the trouble started, I realized as I wrote, and that pleased me.

I wrote my way through talking with Jordan, who I never quite bothered to get over, and March, who was gone now. Queen's General had more terrors than I realized, with the woman in the ceiling and the anatomical beauty, and the paper should have run out, but it didn't. Hearts can hold everything, if you let them. I kept writing, weaving back and forth in a way that likely only made sense to myself. I found myself writing about Hennessey and about Daphne Blackwood, who didn't deserve to be forgotten, because hearts are also inheritances, and I wrote about the blood rinsing down the drain because there are horrors as well.

I wrote back as well as forward, to muster at Fort McCoy and my great-grandmother who loved me because she thought no one else would and the blasted fields of France and the sun rising silver over Cantigny. In a few years, I would be Nick Carraway longer than he had been, and that surely meant something, who I was, what I had done and the people who knew me. I wrote about my mother in St. Paul, my brief time in California and how coming back to New York was a strange kind of relief. If I was unhappy here, at least it might be of a kind I knew I could withstand.

Then I came to New Year's Eve, and though it was August 7th and only early evening on the Scarr River, just beyond the doors, the bells were ringing and people were singing, and it was 1940, a new decade, a new war. Those who survived it would forever mourn the ones who hadn't. Some nights, I wasn't sure what I had survived or if I had. All I knew was that I had made it to midnight, and the clock was chiming, and I was writing, and I couldn't stop, because if I did, I'd come to the end of it, and it would be over and done, and I couldn't stand that, and the door is opening, and I hear a step on the bloodied floor, and a hand on my shoulder, and he—

ACKNOWLEDGMENTS

Unreliable narrators, man. Blixa Bargeld said, "Everything I say is true. Except for the lies." That's it, more or less.

With great thanks to my agent, Diana Fox, who liked this one based on the title alone, and my editors Ruoxi Chen and Sanaa Ali-Virani, who prevent me from falling flat on my face where others can see.

To the folks who actually took this from a pile of words to a thing we can present to all the nice people, Christine Foltzer, Marisa Aragón Ware, Michael Dudding, Alexis Saarela, Sarah Weeks, Lauren Hougen, Steven Bucsok, Greg Collins, Amanda Hong, Dakota Griffin, and Steen Comer, thank you so much!

Cris Chingwa, Victoria Coy, Leah Kolman, and Meredy Shipp, thanks for being you! Please never stop!

For Shane Hochstetler, Grace Palmer, and Carolyn Mulroney, I want to make crepes again, a whole bunch. I have this recipe for citrus preserves I want to try, and I think it'd be great on crepes. Who wants crepes? (Thanks for everything, I love you.)

And for the readers, everyone's telling you a story: everyone who loves you and everyone who hates you. You get to decide what you make of them.

ABOUT THE AUTHOR

NGHI VO is the author of the novels *Siren Queen, The Chosen and the Beautiful,* and *The City in Glass,* as well as the acclaimed novellas of the Singing Hills Cycle, which began with *The Empress of Salt and Fortune.* Her work has been nominated for the Nebula, Locus, and Lambda Literary Awards and the Le Guin Prize, and has won the Crawford, Ignyte, World Fantasy, and Hugo Award. Born in Illinois, she now lives on the shores of Lake Michigan. She believes in the ritual of lipstick, the power of stories, and the right to change your mind.

Website: nghivo.com
Bluesky: nghivo.bsky.social